THE BLACK ROSE OF HALFETI

Modern Middle East Literatures
in Translation Series

the BLACK ROSE *of* HALFETI

a novel by NAZLI ERAY

translated by Robert Finn

CENTER FOR MIDDLE EASTERN STUDIES
The University of Texas at Austin

Printed in the United States of America

Cover image: Courtesy of iStock

Series Editor: Wendy E. Moore

Library of Congress Control Number: 2017932835
ISBN: 978-1-4773-1309-1

Originally published in Turkish as
Halfeti'nin Siyah Gülü by Doğan Kitap in 2012.

THE BLACK ROSE OF HALFETI

Dear Madam,

I am madly in love with you. Maybe that is why I hold your hand in mine for so long and squeeze it so tightly. To feel your touch. I want to sleep with you. I want to make love to you, to make you mine. But Elfe must not hear of this in any way. If we are to make love, you should purchase a drug from a pharmacy. The name of the drug is Viagra. This will take place in your home, if you should be willing. I wait impatiently for that day, the day that you will be mine. My cell phone is 0535 361 77 13. Don't use my home phone. Use this one. If I don't answer, it means I can't talk then. Please don't get the Viagra from a pharmacy near your house. They won't think well of you. Get it from another pharmacy. If I take this medicine, we'll be very happy. Don't forget to destroy this message, sweetheart.

THE SEYR-I MARDIN RESTAURANT

I am sitting on the top floor of the Seyr-i Mardin, looking out at enchanting Mesopotamia spread before me. This city has intoxicated me; I feel as though I had something to drink, but on the contrary, everything around me is perfectly measured, perfectly calm and quiet.

Up above on the hill, Mardin Castle looks out at the plain of Mesopotamia and beyond, as it has done so for centuries.

There's a slight breeze blowing now; my hair flutters, and I readjust the black-framed sunglasses I am wearing.

Down below, a playful Arab tune jammed into a cassette player caresses my ears for a moment or two, then stops. Cut off. Mardin spreads out around me; I look out at this extraordinary city as though enchanted.

Silence.

The silence around me fills my head, making me dizzy. I want to walk some more in the narrow backstreets; I want to go up the nearby staircase and look down. I want to buy scented soap and never leave this city.

And actually, no one asked me, no one invited me here.

The city, silent and reticent, introverted, turned me with that strange energy it radiates into a fly fallen into a spider's web and about to die.

The Seyr-i Mardin.

A high place. I climbed up so many flights of stairs to get here. A setting that offers the city and the plain of Mesopotamia to me where I sit.

I'm both content here and struggling inside that murky, sticky, thick spider web into which I have tumbled.

I suddenly realize that this spider web must be a storm in my soul, the expression of a precipice inside my brain. Mardin, lying here so peacefully with its stone houses, narrow streets, and cool, dark courtyards, has nothing to do with this.

The only thing it did do was turn me into a fly and make me fall into that spider trap that I sheltered inside me.

Now I'm struggling. I'm struggling inside myself.

I could die. I could die as I struggle.

I realize this. I have to be calmer. More calm.

I take a sip from the water in front of me.

I'm calmer now.

A thousand thoughts are passing through my mind.

I realize that I'm in love with Mardin. Whenever I struggle like a fly inside that spider web, I realize that I'm in love. A love so intense it's as though it tore off my wings, broke my hairy fly legs, and blinded me. I can't do a thing.

There is an ancient city before me. I know neither its language nor its geography. I just suddenly showed up here.

It takes me into the palm of its hand, makes me a captive. It won. It won't let me go, let me escape from it . . .

Even though it's so hot, I don't want to leave the Seyr-i Mardin.

I scan Mesopotamia with my eyes as it stretches out in front of me, trying to capture something on the distant line of the horizon.

There's nothing there.

Everything is peaceful and quiet.

That Arab music starts to sound again from somewhere down below.

It's so playful, so lively!

I close my eyes and let myself go with the music for a moment. I relax a little.

I fell in love with a city of stone. There's no one here I know, no place to go, nothing that belongs to me.

If the sun gets hotter, I'll seek shelter in some courtyard and drink some more water.

I'm still listening to the music. The ancient stone city surrounds me. It seems to have taken me by the waist and is drawing me in.

"Let me learn a few streets, and find myself a hotel. A little restaurant, a store that sells soap . . . I have to find these," I was thinking. "A mirror shop, and Shahmerans on mirrors . . . I have to find them. I should get myself a pendant. A silver ring!"

THE MIDNIGHT LETTER

I will not forget for the rest of my life that letter I received at midnight. It was nearly one A.M. in Ankara when I received that cry of longing and passion, that strange, demanding letter, that manifesto of desire. I held the little piece of paper in my trembling fingers, reading in astonishment the sentences written in an agitated and expansive script.

A few minutes before the letter arrived, the following conversation had taken place in the Ankara night:

Elfe spoke excitedly.

"I was in the room inside. I heard banging noises at the door. I took the gun out of the drawer and put a bullet in it. 'Who's there?' I shouted. The racket at the door continued. Just then you called . . ."

"It was like I just felt an urge. That's why I called. How are you?" I asked. "How are you?"

"There's all this noise at the door. It could be a thief. Don't hang up the phone."

"Let me call the police."

"I have a gun."

"Please don't take the gun out. I'm calling the police."

I could hear Elfe speaking on the other end of the phone.

She must have opened the door.

"A, a . . . Doctor! Is that you? I almost shot you . . ."

"What's going on, Elfe?" I shouted from the other end of the phone.

"The doctor came down from the apartment upstairs. He was the one banging on the door. It was hard to see him in the darkness. He came downstairs in his pajamas, the doctor," said Elfe.

I heard the old doctor's voice.

"Where? Where is she?" he asked. "I'm looking for her."

"She's not here. She's in her own house," Elfe said. "But she's on the phone right now."

"I'm worried, very worried about her," the old doctor said. "I'm very worried about her," he repeated.

"Talk to her, she's on the phone."

Elfe gave the phone to the doctor.

"Hello, Doctor Bey?" I said.

"Hello!" said the doctor. "I'm very worried, very worried about you."

"Don't worry, I'm in my house."

"You weren't here."

"I'm at home now."

"A letter," the doctor whispered into the phone. "I wrote you a letter. I came to give it to you."

"I'll get it tomorrow morning."

"I have to leave it tonight," said the doctor. "But Elfe shouldn't see it."

I was a little taken aback. The old doctor was Elfe's upstairs neighbor.

"I left the letter in the box," the doctor said. "The white box next to the door."

I could hear the doctor pacing in the corridor.

"I left the letter in the white box," he said. "Once you've read it, destroy it."

He hung up the phone.

I was thinking, in the semidarkness of my room, What could it be?

I called Elfe again.

She picked up the phone.

"What happened?" I asked.

"Strange," said Elfe. "The old doctor came downstairs; he was the one making the racket at the door. I took out the gun and opened the door. He saw the gun right away. After all, he's a former soldier. He raised his hands in the air. He was asking for you. He was worried. That's what he said. When he talked to you on the phone he seemed to relax a little. He came inside and walked about a little in the corridor. He had his pajamas on . . . I've never seen him like that. I brought him upstairs, to his apartment. His wife is old, and she must have been asleep. I didn't see the caretaker. He left the door open when he came down."

"Elfe, would you look in the white leather box in front of the mirror?"

"I'll take a look; what's there?" said Elfe.

She opened the box.

"There's a piece of paper, a folded-up message here," she said.

"Would you read it to me?"

"Sure."

I listened to Elfe's voice as it came from the other end of the phone.

Dear Madam,

I am madly in love with you. Maybe that is why I hold your hand in mine for so long and squeeze it so tightly. To feel your touch. I want to sleep with you. I want to make love to you, to make you mine. But Elfe must not hear of this in any way. If we are to make love, you should purchase a drug from a pharmacy. The name of the drug is Viagra. This will take place in your home, if you should be willing. I wait impatiently for that day, the day that you will be mine. My cell phone is 0535 361 77 13. Don't use my home phone. Use this one. If I don't answer, it means I can't talk then. Please don't get the Viagra from a pharmacy near your house. They won't think well of you. Get it from another pharmacy. If I take this medicine, we'll be very happy. Don't forget to destroy this message, sweetheart.

The letter the old doctor had left in the box had ripped the Ankara night apart, as though into pieces; it had fallen like a bomb into that sensible, quiet, sleepy darkness of the city night.

I was confused.

The directness of the letter, the commanding tone, everything in it astonished me.

Elfe shouted: "What is this?" from the other end of the phone. "What the hell is this? How can this guy dare to do something like this? I'll tell the building manager. I almost shot him. A lunatic!"

"Quiet," I said. "Please don't say anything to anyone. Nobody should hear about it. Hide the letter. I'll look at it when I come tomorrow. He's a very old man. He must be going through something . . ."

I hung up the phone.

I had no idea what to think, what I should do.

The darkness of that silent, tranquil, subdued Ankara night suddenly seemed to come alive.

For a minute it seemed like there were eyes looking at me through my bedroom curtains. I got up and went into the next room. In the living room, the plants with their green leaves seemed like they were awake. One leaf quivered slightly in the darkness. It had grown a little. It was getting ready for the morning.

I was thinking about the old doctor. His light blue eyes and the sharp lines of his face came before my eyes. I had seen very little of him. I was in a state of confusion.

Two months ago, when I was sitting in the living room, he had come down to Elfe's apartment from the apartment upstairs with his wife.

THE OLD DOCTOR

"Allah, Allah," Elfe whispered into my ear. "I've been living in this apartment for years. This is the first time that the doctor and his wife have come here, come downstairs. Last year the doctor made such a fuss just because I planted linden tree saplings in the garden. And you know, I pulled them out and replanted them next to the wall. He's a grouch. A tough guy.

An old solider. Graduated from two university faculties. He's a pharmacist too. He had an important job for years in a hospital. He's from Izmir."

I saw the old doctor's wife close up for the first time.

We couldn't figure out exactly how old they were, but they must have been at least eighty. We offered them coffee. We had a nice chat.

The clarity of the doctor's mind astounded us. He was telling us about things that had happened years ago, when he first came from Izmir to Ankara . . . the old Gülhane hospital, some of the streets in Ankara that were still dirt roads then, told us about the Ankara they had come to as a young couple, and about Izmir. He was a tall, thin man, the old doctor. His wife's caretaker had slipped into a corner and was listening to what the doctor said.

His wife was silent. It was clear that she had once been a very beautiful woman.

The visit of these very old people had both surprised and pleased us.

Elfe said: "These are grand people; who knows how many years they've carried on, who knows what they've seen and been though in their lives? For people like them to just show up here out of the blue like that is both weird and somehow good fortune, a little bit of luck, if you ask me. Like swallows coming in from the balcony of an old mansion in spring and fluttering from here to there under the high ceiling . . ."

"Right," I said. "Today's an unusual day. What a different world these old people told us about. So, they're from Izmir?"

"From Izmir. Both the doctor and his wife are from Izmir," said Elfe.

I was amazed by the old doctor's memory. He was the master of an older world, I felt it.

He spoke about old Izmir, of Alsancak, of Kordonboyu, and Kemeraltı.

IZMIR

I love this city; I know it like the palm of my hand. The place that makes me the most nostalgic is the Military Cemetery on Kadifekale. In this dynamic, lively city full of activity, I am profoundly affected by those silent, solemn tombstones, that organized state of death, the green shadows of the trees in the cemetery, and the fact that all these people removed from the world are now just a part of the earth, each but a name written upon a stone.

But Izmir is teeming with life. It's like an uncontrollable, sexy woman. For me, Izmir is a woman preparing little meze snacks for her lover in front of a small window that looks out on the sea, cutting melon into slices and lining them up in a little boat-shaped plate, someone who doesn't wear a bra under her thin print summer dress, with slightly plump arms, whose permanent has grown out, the blonde ends gathered at the back of her neck by a clip with gemstones on it, someone who has one or two thin gold bracelets on her arm, whose name might be something like Müzeyyen. Full of life, of hope, waiting at the window for her man, maybe sitting on his lap with her incredibly soft hips when he comes, someone who has the softness of the women from the old days, from childhood, a woman who occasionally hums a song, Müzeyyen.

Izmir. Izmir that I love so much. A boat slowly oozes its way across to Karşıyaka, as I sit sipping my tea in the little café at Pasaport.

Müzeyyen, you're so beautiful at this time of the evening. I want to jump on the boat and go over to Karşıyaka; I want to get into the carriage of an old driver and clip-clop through the streets of Güzelyalı. I want the Gypsy fortuneteller in Susuz Dede (Thirsty Grandpa) Park, over by Fahrettin Altay's place, to fling her beans down on the stone in front of me and say sweet lies that sound lovely to my ears.

The fortuneteller talks on her cell phone every once in a while. I look and see that the phone in her hand is not a bad model at all.

"Are you Esin Moralıoğlu?" she asks me. "I swear, you look just like her. Your hair's so pretty."

She tosses the stones in front of me.

"What's this stone?"

"It's Tayyip. It's a good luck stone. The good luck stone came to you."

I look at the fortuneteller's face. It's like charcoal. Black. Her hair has henna in it. She ties the scarf on her head on the side, and throws the beans, the tokens down in front of me again.

"What's this one?" I say.

"It's an old man," she says. "He's in love with you. He won't give up. Girl, are you under a spell? There's a spell on you. Give me a hundred liras, and I'll break it."

"I don't want that, I don't, I don't want the spell to be broken!" I say.

The fortuneteller opens her eyes wide.

"Girl, are you crazy? They've got you all tied up. You don't get to be with your lover . . . To get back together, to have your feet touch one another again . . . The man is old. But he has money . . . Wait a minute . . ."

"That's enough," I say.

I throw some money down in front of the Gypsy woman and stand up.

"You're crazy," says the woman. "All around you are mountains, stones, earth. Let me break it and you can let go and relax."

"I like to live like that."

"Really?"

"Really," I say.

"I've never heard of people like you," says the fortuneteller. "I'm here. If you change your mind, come back. I'll break the spell, rip everything up. I'll cut those ropes that bind you to pieces."

I listen to her with interest.

"My soul is bound . . ."

"Let me release it, girl. What have I been saying to you?"

"Don't change it. Leave it like this. Let me stay bound."

I leave Susuz Dede Park.

Müzeyyen, you're so beautiful! The bay sloshes around your plump white knees. In the sky, the bright half-moon has come out.

I could go mad. Everything all around me is so beautiful.

I'm a stranger in this city, actually. I don't even have a place to stay. This is the old doctor's city.

THE ZINCIRIYE HOTEL
MARDIN

I closed the curtains in my room in the Zinciriye Hotel. There were colorful kilims on the floor, and in the corner a couch with brightly striped satin cushions on it. My bed had been turned down.

Outside was Mardin.

The night air was a little cool. I walked under the archway in the stone room and looked out the window on the other side, into the darkness. The roads were silent, and I saw trembling lights in the side streets. The sound of music came to me again from somewhere, as though there were a musical evening someplace close by. Mesopotamia lay before me, quiet and still.

I was inside the night of Mardin. All alone with myself. I leaned back on the silk pillows and took a sip of the rose sherbet in front of me.

This city gave me a strange tranquility. As though I were a hundred years old. I knew everything; I'd lived it all and forgotten it. I felt that kind of lightness. I took another sip from the rose sherbet with lemon.

From the edge of the window I could see part of the Şehidiye Mosque in the lights of the minarets.

In a little while I'd lie down on my bed and drift off to sleep. Or I might curl up on the sofa where I was sitting. I could bury my head among the silk pillows. My eyelids were slowly getting heavier. A silver ring with a purple stone that I had seen in the underground market during the day came to mind. It was so beautiful.

I wondered if I'd be able to find that store tomorrow.

It was somewhere over there by the Seyr-i Mardin.

I heard a noise by my ear. Like a cat purring. I quickly turned my head. I came nose to nose with a dark man. He was closely examining me with his deep black eyes, a rather ugly man whom I seemed to know from somewhere, but how could someone get into my room at this hour of the night?

I jumped up from where I had been curled up. I was all set to yell as loud as I could, to let out a scream.

The man slowly put his finger up to his lips and signaled me to be quiet.

He was well dressed, wearing an olive-colored jacket with an open-necked white shirt underneath. He was unshaven and had purple rings under his eyes. His hands were long and his fingers bony.

"What do you want here?" I asked. "Who are you?"

"You don't recognize me . . . ," said the man.

"I don't know you! And what do you want in my hotel at this hour?"

The man replied calmly:

"I'm Luis Buñuel. The man you always think about. Or at least that's what I thought. But see, you didn't even recognize me . . ."

I was befuddled.

I scrutinized him very carefully now.

Yes, it was. The man across from me was indeed the famous Spanish director Luis Buñuel. I suddenly recognized him. The photograph on the cover of the book in my house that I never put down . . . *My Last Breath*. The Spanish genius I so admired. The man I got so excited about when I read his autobiography. Someone I might desire to be with if he were alive.

He was a close friend of the French surrealists, Sartre, Camus, Pablo Neruda, and Salvador Dali. Luis Buñuel, with whom the poet Federico Garcia Lorca was in love. There he was across from me among the multicolored silk cushions in my room with the stone arch in the Zinciriye Hotel in Mardin.

He was an incredible man, an expert at passion and perversion, who could extract the human spirit like a liqueur from a still and masterfully explain it, male to the core, who played with guns, wandered in graveyards, and deafened himself in one ear by firing off a gun in an enclosed room.

In Mardin . . .

In my hotel room.

"Mr. Buñuel, I do recognize you," I said. "Please excuse me; I just couldn't place you a minute ago. Tired from the trip . . . The influence of this city . . ."

"But what a city," muttered Luis Buñuel. "The city out there is incomparable. It's very different from Toledo and Madrid, but it still has such a similar atmosphere."

"Yes," I cried. "Toledo!"

"And Madrid," said Buñuel. "Here and there. The Madrid I live in and suffered with. Like in a dream . . . Bits and pieces."

I had read that he was very short tempered. The famous star Catherine Deneuve had written in an elegant little book her memories of the films she made with him and expressed how intimidated she was by Buñuel. Buñuel didn't even speak to the star, who was in the lead role; some days were harder to work with him, he was very exacting and sometimes spent days on tiny details. Still, Catherine Deneuve admired him. She played the lead in his films *Belle de Jour* and *Tristana*.

"His hearing difficulties sometimes made it impossible to communicate with him," she wrote in one part of the book.

"His genius was amazing. It was hard to meet his demands. He was a deep, silent man."

I was so jealous when I read these sentences of Catherine Deneuve's . . . to work with Luis Buñuel. To go into his world, to be able to experience the unreachable power of his imagination and the pitch-black labyrinths of his subconscious. To be near him, as he analyzed life . . .

"What are you thinking?" asked Buñuel.

"The things that I know about you. What I was able to learn . . ."

"Really?" he said. I realized that he was thinking about completely different things.

"Tell me," he said, leaning over toward me. "What did you feel when you read that midnight letter the old doctor wrote to you?"

"How do you know about that letter?" I burst out, astonished.

"I know," said Buñuel. "I know this letter full of desire and obsession very well. You're hiding it in your purse, in your business card case."

I was amazed.

"How can you know all of these details? The inside of my purse?"

He chuckled.

"There's a wonderful photograph of Marilyn Monroe on your card case. You had that case made in Giresun this year . . ."

My mouth was agape.

"Yes," I muttered. "I had that case made when I went to Giresun. Marilyn's picture is on it. And the letter is inside. But you . . . How can you know such details?"

"It's my job to know details," said Buñuel. "Pay it no mind."

He drew close to me and stared into my eyes.

"Why didn't you throw that letter away? Why are you still keeping it in your card case? You could have ripped it up and thrown it away that night. But you didn't throw it away;

you're keeping it," he said. "Why? Tell me, why?"

I couldn't answer the question.

"I don't know why myself," I murmured. "Maybe to read it again. All my life I always ripped up interesting letters that I received and threw them away. Maybe that's why I kept this letter . . ."

"A letter that comes from an eighty-six-year-old man," said Buñuel.

"Yes, it's an interesting letter," I said. "It completely exposes the male subconscious."

Buñuel nodded.

"Yes, it's very interesting," he said. "Extraordinary, actually. Well that could be the subject for a film."

Why hadn't I thrown away the letter that the old doctor had put in the white letter box at Elfe's house after rushing downstairs in his pajamas in the middle of the night?

I asked myself, "Why?"

Buñuel's eyes were fixed on me.

"Don Luis," I said. "As I said, I couldn't throw that letter out because it exposed a man's subconscious, stark, unexplored. Not everyone gets a letter like that. There are strange things in that midnight letter: insistence, an order, a forceful passion, and perversion. I couldn't have thrown all of that into the garbage."

"Right," said Buñuel. "The letter is a document. In your hands. That old doctor actually placed a map of his soul in your hands. A document of passion."

"A document of passion," I muttered.

I felt a sense of incredible excitement being there with Buñuel.

"Do you want to see the letter?" I asked.

"If you have no objection, yes," he said.

I went through my purse, which was on the table, and found my card case. From the cover, Marilyn was winking at me with her sexiest look.

"Here, here's the letter."

I took out the little smudged piece of paper and gave it to Buñuel. He took it from my hand and carefully read the sentences that the old doctor had written.

"Let me order you a rose sherbet."

"Okay."

I pressed the buzzer. A little later there was a tap on the door; it was the waiter. I slowly opened the door in the entryway of my room, beyond the arch, a little crack.

"I'd like another glass of rose sherbet."

"Of course, ma'am. Should I put a little cinnamon in it?"

"Please do."

I went back into the room.

Luis Buñuel held the letter out to me.

"It's an extraordinary sexual passion," he said. "Where is this man now?"

"In Ankara; he lives on the top floor of the building my friend lives in."

"Where does he observe you from?"

"I don't know," I said.

"Most likely from a window," said Buñuel.

There was a knock at the door. I went and got the rose sherbet.

"Drink this."

"Is it good?"

"You'll like it . . ."

"Thank you," said Buñuel.

He took a sip of the rose sherbet.

"This is like the very city we're in," he said. "Mysterious. Wonderful."

I remembered the big living room window above the street door. The old doctor sat there sometimes.

"He sees you from that world every day; he follows you," said Luis Buñuel.

The call to prayer drifting out over all Mardin from the

minaret of the Şehidiye Mosque interrupted our conversation briefly. Then the call to prayer coming from the other mosques seemed to be echoing off the stone walls.

Buñuel finished off his rose sherbet in one gulp.

He had stood up.

"Are you going?" I asked.

"I am," he said. "I'll come again. It's very late. I'll go to Diyarbakır tomorrow. In the afternoon I'll come back to Mardin."

"You're going to Diyarbakır?" I asked in surprise.

"Yes," he said. "I have to meet someone in the Sülüklü Han. You'll still be here, right?"

"I'm here," I said. "I'll be in my room tomorrow afternoon, Don Luis."

"See you then," he said.

I rushed to the door after he left. I opened it and stared for a long time at the hall spread with green, blue, and red kilims. He must have left quickly. The corridor was empty and the hotel was asleep.

I went back in my room and locked the door. I curled up on the couch. It must be almost morning. So that meant Buñuel had stayed in my room a long time.

I looked at the empty glass of the rose sherbet he had drunk down.

My eyes were slowly closing.

THE WINDOW IN ANKARA

I was about to go into Elfe's apartment, on Meneviş Street, as I do every afternoon. I had gotten out of the taxi a second or two ago, and I was putting my change purse into my big handbag as I raised my eyes and looked up.

He's always there in the window. Sometimes sitting, sometimes standing, the woman who takes care of him sitting in the chair nearby.

The old doctor was looking down from the window at me,

smiling slightly. I seemed to see a strange gleam, like that of happiness, in his cold blue eyes.

Ever since I got that letter, I've found myself ineluctably looking up at that window now and then.

I raised my eyes a little, and I was met with that pair of pale blue eyes staring at me. I went inside with quick steps, sometimes even running, and quickly pressed Elfe's bell one or two times.

Elfe opened the door.

"Your guy's in the window again."

"When did you see him?" I asked.

"A little while ago, when I went out to get *simits* for you. He was waiting there."

"Waiting for what? How would he know what time I was going to come?"

"He just knows," said Elfe. "You always come around the same time. He sits down in front of the window before noon."

"There's a woman who takes care of him . . ."

"She's there for his wife," said Elfe.

"What if he comes downstairs again?"

"Then I'll tell the building manager."

"Don't, that would be a terrible thing!"

"They should control him. He's obviously sneaking out of the house," said Elfe.

"Do you think that's normal?"

"How could it be normal? He's senile. He probably has Alzheimer's."

"But when they came down here and were talking to us, there was nothing wrong. Well, there was nothing definite," I said.

"It could have just happened all of a sudden," said Elfe. "We hear him. He's talking up there."

"But if that's the case, it's awful," I said.

"I think the caretaker is perfectly aware of everything. She's always with the doctor there at the window. She says some things to him."

"I doubt it," I said. "He laid down the condition that you shouldn't hear about anything in the letter he sent me."

"The guy is senile," said Elfe. "Disgusting. Those thoughts . . ."

"But this is only a manifestation. An aged brain manifesting a desire . . ."

Elfe just kept staring at me.

"It's a really gross, audacious, awful thing."

"I know. Like the subconscious of the old people in Buñuel's films," I muttered.

"Who's Buñuel?"

"Luis Buñuel. A surrealist. A Spanish director. I adore him. I'll show you one of his films the first chance I get," I said.

"Are there things like this in his films?"

"Things like this . . . and more. Very unusual."

Elfe shook her head.

"Luis Buñuel," she said. "Is he alive?"

"No. He died. If he were alive, I'd find him. I adore him. I'm fixated," I said.

"Was he handsome?"

"He was an ugly man."

"I'm curious," said Elfe. "Let's watch one of his films."

"Fine, I'll bring one of his films over. *Viridiana* or *Tristana*."

"Where will you find it?"

"There's a video shop on the bottom floor of the shopping arcade in Tunalı Hilmi where the movie theater used to be."

"Okay."

PHYSICAL IMPRISONMENT

I was slowly climbing up the narrow zigzag stairs with iron railings on the side to get to the Seyr-i Mardin. The inside of my hand had rust on it; I'd wipe it off when I got up there. Who knows where I had wandered?

Finally I got up to the very top and reached the terrace up there.

The view in front of me was dizzying.

Silent, mysterious Mesopotamia stretched out to the edge of the horizon, where it seemed to meet Syria.

The colors were always the same. A world of grey, beige, and light brown. In front of me were a few houses with flat roofs, and one or two unusual minarets. The air was cloudless and dry. There was a glow in the sky today, a secret track of the sun that seemed to show the plain in a different way.

I sat down on a chair at the edge of the terrace, next to the iron railing, looking at the horizon and at the nearby surroundings. I could see things today that I couldn't see yesterday. I saw a little graveyard next to a tiny mosque. Silent and alone. A haze slowly started to form in the air, like some kind of thin dust descending. I realized that the weather was getting warmer.

I drifted off in thought.

The body as a prison.

I was imprisoned within my own body. This city, this atmosphere and the world I encountered here for the first time that was so unusual, so out of the ordinary, made me think of this.

I was imprisoned in my body, by my eyes, whether sharp or myopic, my legs, weak or strong, by what I could reach with my two hands, the steps I took, the body I carried, my little aches and pains, my weariness, my lack of energy or the opposite feeling I sometimes had of extreme vitality, the swelling in my left foot, the ache in my left knee, the slight ringing in my ear, and the burning in my chest, all of these imprisoned me in my body. A soul confined in a body.

I slowly started to be aware of this physical confinement that I had never noticed in the early years of my life.

Was it a bad thing?

Absolutely not. This was me, with my aching tooth, lazy eye, my stomach that sometimes filled with gas, it was me, and I was a person made out of flesh and bone.

All these things that I have enumerated were things that reminded me of my existence and that I was alive. The moment I was released from the prison of my physical being, I would be dead.

I suddenly realized that. My soul would leave the home it had had for years, go someplace else, and maybe to some new home where it would settle itself, try to find a brand-new fate for itself. I asked the waiter for cold water and a coffee with mastic in it.

The plain of Mesopotamia and Mardin made me think of these things.

Maybe the city made me feel the presence of the sheikhs and dervishes that could be abstracted out of its body.

Its influence over me was extraordinary. As I experienced it, as I followed it for days and nights, I seemed to be constantly in dialogue with a kind of wisdom.

"I am content," I said. "I'm content with this imprisonment by the body."

My eye was attracted to the old cemetery on the slope of the ancient mosque. The bodies lying there had all been abandoned, left to the earth.

So, that's what was passing through my mind as I sat on the terrace on the top floor of the Seyr-i Mardin.

Imprisoned by the body.

"Anyway, one day this confinement will end; you'll be let out," said a voice next to my ear.

I quickly turned and looked. There was no one there. I looked behind me, nobody there.

I must have imagined I heard something, I thought to myself.

There was no one around.

The waiter had vanished too.

I slowly sipped my water. If I asked for a rose sherbet, would they have it, I wondered, around here?

Somebody was coming up the stairs. I heard his footsteps. It must be some tourist visiting the city. The place where I sat was one of the most attractive locations in the city. But this place was not a touristic city. It had remained beautiful and mysterious because it was untouched; it had withdrawn and protected itself.

Suddenly I thought of that purple ring. The ring with the purple stone I saw in the window of a shop in the underground market yesterday morning. I had to buy it.

The person climbing up the steps of the Seyr-i Mardin appeared now. He came over to me.

It was Luis Buñuel!

"Don Luis," I called out excitedly. "Is that you? I heard your footsteps."

I immediately pulled a chair over next to me. He came and sat down.

"The stairs were steep and exhausting, but it's worth it to see this view," he said.

His eyes were sweeping over the plain of Mesopotamia.

Who knew what the city was making him think?

Suddenly I remembered. "You were supposed to go to Diyarbakır today," I said.

"Yes, I had something to do there, but I put it off," he said. "I wandered around in Mardin and I looked for you. In the end I guessed that you would be here. I want to ask you some things."

I ordered rose sherbets from the waiter.

"Please put cinnamon in it," I said.

"Yes, ma'am."

"There were things I wanted to ask," Buñuel continued. "Things about the old doctor. Did he seem quite normal the last time you spoke to him?"

"I only spoke to him once anyway. He seemed perfectly

normal to me," I said. "In other words, there was nothing strange in what he said or how he talked. He remembered everything very well. In fact, I was surprised at how powerful his memory was. He spoke about what Ankara and Izmir were like in the old days. We spoke about this and that, regular things, too. Everything seemed normal."

Buñuel took a sip from the rose sherbet the waiter had brought.

"In other words, he didn't show any symptoms of Alzheimer's," he said.

"I don't understand. Do you think the old doctor has Alzheimer's?"

"I don't know," said Buñuel. "I wonder about it. He might not either . . ."

"But a letter like that, the audacity, coming downstairs in the middle of the night, that declaration of love?"

He shook his head. He was thinking.

"Maybe he's in the first phases of the disease," he said. "He recognizes you, knows himself, knows his desire and easily communicates it. There are orders and directions in the letter. There's no disconnect, nothing missing."

"Yes," I said. "I noticed that too."

"As though he were used to commanding . . ."

"He was apparently an eminent doctor. A stern man," I said. "Everyone in the hospital was terrified of him, I guess."

"He was a stern man."

Buñuel was intrigued.

"Very tough," I said. "In the apartment where he lives now, he gets involved in all kinds of things, giving orders, like all the old retired people. But I can imagine him in the hospital, when he was young."

I had finished my rose sherbet. In some indescribable way it quenched my thirst and cooled me.

"So you've thought about him when he was young," said Buñuel.

I was taken aback for a moment.

"Yes, I did," I said. "Really, I imagined it."

"That's so interesting," said Buñuel. "It's so interesting that you thought about that . . ."

I blushed a little.

"Why?" I asked. "Why is it interesting that I thought about his youth?"

"You're imagining what he was like years ago," said Buñuel. "That proposal that came to you in the middle of the night. An old man over eighty, useless now. You would probably be afraid if you were left alone with him."

"That's for sure," I said.

"A masculine spirit, trapped in an aged body. A brain that may or may not be working very well. And you're an obsession in that brain now," he said.

"Yes," I agreed softly.

"It's not important how the brain functions or doesn't," said Buñuel. "The really important thing is that you're inside that brain. You're there now. In fact right now, at this very moment as you sit here on this terrace in Mardin, you're inside that man's brain. You're an image, a voice, an object of desire, someone he's waiting for."

"It's a terrible thing," I said. "Revolting. What can I do?"

"Nothing," said Buñuel.

"If the old doctor has Alzheimer's, he might forget me," I said.

"Maybe he'll remember only you," said Buñuel.

"How do you know?"

"I know the male soul," he said. "You know my films . . ."

"I know," I said. "It's like a clip taken from one of your films."

He laughed a little.

"I'm aware of that," he said in a low voice.

"Is that why you're here, Don Luis? Are you here to follow this matter from up close?"

"Maybe," he said.

He had stood up.

"Now I'll go down those incredibly steep steps," he said.

"Are you leaving?"

"I'll come and find you again," he said. He walked off toward the stairs.

I sat there for a while. I gazed at the vast, endless plain in front of me, at the light slipping out from between the clouds and making plays of color on the plain, and the line of the little graveyard, and the hazy sky in the distance.

IZMIR

How did I get here?

I was confused.

It was as though I had been flung into the sky like a ball, and splat! landed here.

I was in Izmir.

Izmir was all around me. It must be just evening; there wasn't a single light lit on the edge of the bay yet. A strange Izmir. A different Izmir.

I looked around. I was somewhere over by Varyant. In front of me was an old building the color of cooked meat that I always used to see; across from me the bay stretched out, filled with the sea, like a blue oyster shell.

There was something strange, the underpasses weren't there, the bridges weren't there, the silhouettes of the big hotels reaching into the sky weren't there; everything was very plain and spare, like some old-time Izmir. I must be in an old Izmir. I suddenly realized this. The city around me was like the Izmir you see in some old postcard. Solitary and absolutely empty.

I started to run down from Varyant in excitement. Am I in a dream? I wondered. But no, everything was very real. The sky was real, the bay was realistic, and there was very little traffic. The bay hadn't been filled in; it was there before me the way it used to be long ago. Maybe it was the Izmir of the sixties that I was in now. I had never seen Izmir in the sixties. I was thinking it must be those years. Completely empty. Like a provincial town.

What could have happened? How did I wind up here? It could also be the seventies. I just can't figure it out. It could also be the fifties, I think to myself now. The old days . . . No crowds, nobody out on the streets. There are beautiful houses along the Kordonboyu waterfront, all of them right on the bay. I ran over there. My foot twisted. My shoe flew off my foot. I fell forward, head over heels. There was an unbelievable pain in my left ankle. A taxi stopped next to me. Tears came from my eyes; I was confused. How did I wind up in this weird world? And if something happens to my ankle . . .

The driver got out of the car and came over to me.

"Are you okay?" he asked. "Can you get up?"

"I can't stand on my foot."

"Let me take you to the hospital," said the driver.

Leaning on his arm, I got into the car.

"Which hospital are we going to?"

"There's a hospital," he said. "Nearby. Konak Maternity."

"Let's go to the emergency room."

I was covered with sweat because of the pain. The car glided down from Varyant in the Izmir twilight. I lay back in the car, observing an Izmir I didn't know at all.

"Here we are."

I got out of the taxi in front of the hospital with the driver's help. I virtually dragged myself over to the door of the emergency room.

A short hospital orderly came out. He was a dark, burly man. He saw me and came running over. I took his arm and went inside.

"Sit there," he said to me. "The doctor will come in a minute."

"Is there an orthopedist? I guess it's broken."

"There's the emergency doctor. He'll examine you."

I stared into the hospital, at this little room at the entrance. You could hear the call to prayer in the distance. It must be the evening prayer.

"The doctor's coming," said the man.

I got to my feet.

A man burst in the door like the wind. He was a tall, thin man.

I looked at his face.

The doctor! It was that doctor! The one in Ankara. The old man who left me the letter in the middle of the night. I stared in amazement at his face. He was very young. He must have been twenty-six or twenty-seven. He looked at me briefly.

"What's the problem?"

"My left ankle . . ."

"How did it happen? Where did you fall?"

"I tripped on the road."

"Were you dizzy?"

"Maybe . . ."

He was examining my ankle with his hand.

"They should do an x-ray," he said. "Take her on a stretcher."

He didn't seem to recognize me.

The attendant jumped up. A little later, I was being carried downstairs on a stretcher that was like a hammock.

So the doctor was in this hospital. Maybe he was an intern. He just showed me a doctor's cold professional interest. This was not the man who had written that letter burning with desire and put it in the mailbox at midnight in Ankara.

What year were we in? I was so curious. I had to find a mirror. I had to look at my face, at my eyes. I started to be curious about myself.

A technician was preparing to take the x-ray. The primitiveness of the equipment astonished me.

"Please put your leg out like that. Slowly . . ."

I stuck my leg out where the technician told me. The squat attendant was by my side. He hadn't left me. I looked at my shoes. They were the black patent leather spring shoes with low heels I had put on this morning in Ankara. My stocking was ripped. My left knee was a little bruised.

"Is there anything wrong with the knee?" the technician asked.

"The doctor didn't look at the knee," the orderly replied.

"Let's take an x-ray of the knee too," said the technician. "Look, it's bruised."

The procedure took a long time. I stared at the ceiling from where I lay.

I wonder what year we are in. What month? How are my face and my eyes? How old am I?

I really wondered about this for a while. I couldn't ask anyone. I couldn't ask what year we were in either.

"How's my ankle?" I was able to ask.

"The doctor will look at the films now," said the technician. "They'll take you upstairs. Sit up slowly."

I raised myself up and sat on the leather cushion. The stretcher, whose middle part swayed like a hammock, arrived. The attendant and a young man lifted me onto the stretcher. We went upstairs through shadowy staircases. The lights slowly started to come on in the hospital. They were dim bulbs that only slightly illuminated the faces of a few people passing by in the corridor before subsiding into an enigmatic semi-darkness inside themselves. I was inside a color that was like a person's past.

We came to the doctor's office. I sat down across from him in a worn-out chair with the attendant's help.

The young man gave the x-rays to the doctor. He was examining them now.

"There's a fracture in the ankle," he said, looking at me.

Those cold blue eyes and his youthful state astounded me.

"Is it broken?" I burst out.

"It's broken but it's a clean break. We'll put a cast on it right away."

He put the x-rays aside.

"What's your name?" he asked.

I said my name, staring into his eyes. He was writing something on a piece of paper with a fountain pen.

"After the cast you can go home. Don't walk on it for three weeks."

"I don't have a home," I murmured.

The doctor was taken aback.

"You don't have a home?"

"I'm not from Izmir."

"I see."

He was thinking.

"I can put you in a bed in a ward of the hospital for a day or two. Would you like that?"

"Yes, that would be fine."

"Well then, let me arrange for a bed in the ward."

He turned to the orderly. "Have them put the cast on. I'll see her in the general surgery ward," he said.

MARDIN

I came to my hotel, passing by the front of the Şehidiye Mosque. I had wandered around in the market and got some rose-scented soap for myself.

There was a melancholy coffin resting on the funeral stone in the courtyard of the mosque. It must be the funeral of a soldier who had been killed. A mother and a beautiful young girl I surmised was the fiancée were weeping next to the coffin.

The sound of someone in the back reading the Kuran came to my ears. The funeral procession started to leave. It was passing right by me now, and I read the name on the casket.

"Sergeant Süleyman Şahin."

Sergeant Süleyman Şahin was lost to sight at the corner. I got to my hotel by walking amid the people following the funeral procession, and went in.

I took out the card from my pocket and opened the door.

The evening sun filled the room. There was a little fan at work inside. The white curtains with embroidered borders were open.

There was a blonde sitting on the couch with the satin pillows. I was bowled over with surprise for a minute.

The blonde was someone I didn't know. She had a graceful figure, straight blonde hair, and a delicate face. Her long legs were gathered beneath her. She rose a little from where she was sitting when she saw me.

"Who are you?" I whispered. "Just who are you?"

"I'm Silvia Pinal," said the blonde.

"Silvia Pinal."

I had never heard this name before.

"Silvia Pinal?"

"Yes," said the blonde. "Haven't you ever heard my name?"

"I may have," I said. "Forgive me. I'm a little detached these days. It might be from the heat. Where do I know you from, I wonder?"

The blonde was sitting up on the couch now, and crossed her legs. She had an innocent but cold face.

"I act in Buñuel's films," she said. "I played in *Viridiana*. An old man's niece who wanted to become a nun . . ."

I suddenly recalled her. She was an extraordinary actress. She had a strange, unfeeling face, as though she were half asleep . . . She played a sleepwalker in *Viridiana*. The young niece who came to her uncle's farm. The old man madly in love with her . . . The rich uncle who hanged himself from a tree when the young niece refused his proposal of marriage.

It was one of Buñuel's strangest films, and the one that affected me the most. A film made in 1961 in Spain.

"I remember you!" I said. "You're Viridiana. You were wonderful!"

"Thank you," said the blonde, with a demure smile.

"I came to your room thinking I'd see Luis," she said. "I know that he comes here."

"Buñuel? Yes, he stopped by here yesterday."

"Would you say that he'd come again today?" she asked.

"I have no idea," I said. "I just see him all of a sudden. Before me, next to me. Like an apparition, but real. We talk a little, and then he goes."

Silvia Pinal was listening to me closely.

"That's the way Luis is," she said. "He suddenly appears next to someone like a protecting angel, or the Angel of Death. A person is afraid of him, feels shy. That kind of man. It's curious that he came to your room at night."

"You probably weren't expecting that he would come to my bedroom at night," I said.

"But he did, didn't he?"

The woman suddenly started to annoy me.

"Yes, he did," I said. "But I have a story. That's why he came."

Silvia Pinal laughed out loud. Her face, her manner, that cold demeanor all suddenly changed.

"Don't get mad," she said. "I'm just joking. I guessed you had a story. I know that's why Luis came here."

"How did you find me here?" I asked.

"Just the same way Luis did," she said.

She had sunk down into the silk pillows.

"It must be an interesting story," she murmured.

"It's not such an interesting thing at all," I said. "An aged doctor left a letter for me in the middle of the night, filled with love, passion, and desire. That's all."

The woman was listening intently to me.

"What more do you want!" she exclaimed. "It's an incredible story. Luis loved it."

"Yes," I said. "He was quite interested."

"It was just his kind of thing," said Silvia Pinal. "Was the man very old?"

"Very old," I said. "On top of that he might have Alzheimer's disease. This proposal he made is unbalanced. If you ask me, he's going through something."

"He may be going through something, but if he's written a love letter, it means there's something real in this . . ."

"A letter filled with passion and desire," I said.

"Sex at that age?" said Silvia Pinal.

"He wrote the name of a drug in the letter too. He wants me to get that medicine from a pharmacy," I said.

"But this is incredible!" said Silvia Pinal. "Extraordinary. Now I understand why Luis was so interested in it. Do you know this old doctor well?"

"I don't know him at all. That's the strange thing about it," I said. "I've seen him once or twice, but that was in the staircase in the apartment building. He came with his wife and care-taker for a visit to my friend's house."

"He came for you," said Silvia Pinal. "He came to see you more closely, to hear what you had to say, to try to explain himself to you at least a little."

"Look, that's right," I said. "The doctor came downstairs for that reason that day. I wasn't able to figure out why they made the visit. Because they hardly go out anywhere. Old people . . ."

"As I said," replied Silvia Pinal, "to be near you . . ."

"You're interested in this story too," I said.

"You have no idea how interested I am."

"Really?" I asked in astonishment. "It just seemed like an ordinary sad story to me."

"It's really not any ordinary story," said the woman. "It interests me, because I might play you in the film."

"What film?" I asked, confused.

The woman stared into my face for a minute.

"The film that Luis Buñuel will direct," she said.

"What film?"

"You were just explaining the story a minute ago. Well, that film."

"Where did it come from that the story I told you is going to be a film?"

"Buñuel's after the story. It's perfectly clear that he's going to have it turned into a scenario and make a film out of the story. And I'm his favorite actress," she said. "So then I'll play the lead; in other words, you."

I was annoyed.

"Miss Pinal," I said. "Nothing has been said about anything like this. And besides, this is my private life. I don't want it to be the subject of a film."

"But you told it to Buñuel," said the woman.

"He knew it anyway. He asked me questions," I said. "But he didn't say anything about a film. Something like that is simply out of the question. I won't give permission."

"Excuse me," said the woman. "I've upset you. I'm going. This is your time to relax . . ."

I didn't make a sound.

Silvia Pinal got herself up from amidst the silk cushions. She fixed her hair a bit with one hand.

"Good day," she said. She opened the door of the room and left. I ran after her, opened the door, and looked out. She must have gotten on the elevator. The corridor was empty.

IZMIR

My left ankle was placed in a cast. I was lying in a twelve-person ward, in a narrow bed at the end.

"Tell us if it hurts."

"What will you do?"

"I'll have them give you a needle," the attendant said. "I know the nurse. Nurse Muazzez."

Actually, I did have pain.

"Can you do that without asking the doctor?"

"The doctor said they should do it if there's pain," he said.

"Then let them go ahead and do it," I said.

The ward was filled with women.

"They've all had hernia operations," said the attendant. "This is the Women's Ward. First Surgical Ward. The doctor was lucky to find a bed. These wards are filled to bursting . . ."

A little later Nurse Muazzez came in with a hypodermic needle in her hand. It was an old glass one.

"Turn your back," she said to me.

She gave me the needle in the thigh. The medicine burned like poison.

"It'll go away in a minute," said the nurse.

She was a beautiful young woman. Blonde, with light-colored eyes.

"Let me check your temperature," she said.

She waved a thermometer and put it under my arm.

"The doctor is coming!"

It was as though a whisper had floated up into the air of the ward and then settled down again. The doctor was at the door.

I turned slightly from where I lay and looked straight at him.

Cold blue eyes, that same height and appearance. Old age often changes people. I tried to see the changes that the last sixty years had made in the physique of the man across from me. The only differences were that in old age his hair was snow white and his movements were slower.

The doctor came over to my bed in two steps.

"How are you?"

"I'm fine, Doctor."

I was staring into his blue eyes. I couldn't detect the slightest indication at all that he knew me, that he had seen me before. A stranger, a young doctor, the hospital ward in old Izmir, and the short, dark attendant observing everything from the side . . .

"Is your bed comfortable?"

"Very comfortable."

"I'll have them put a pillow under your ankle so it doesn't swell," he said.

He lifted the sheet covering my ankle and examined the cast.

"Is the cast too tight?"

"A little."

"Yes, they made it a little tight. If it bothers you a lot, I'll have them cut it."

The nurse had come. She seemed livelier standing next to the doctor. Their expressions were different.

"What medicine are you giving?"

"The ones you prescribed, sir."

The doctor turned to me.

"Are you able to sleep?" he asked.

"I'll try," I said.

"When you have pain, let them give you a painkiller. The nurse will do it. I might prescribe something for you to have during the night."

"Thank you."

"Be well."

The doctor left the ward like an arrow in flight.

The orderly bent down to my ear.

Slowly, he said:

"Everyone's sick over this guy. All the women."

"Really?"

"Really. He's a real lady's man."

He suddenly became quiet. The women in the ward were talking from one bed to another.

Their voices were soft and relaxing, like the chirping of finches put out on the balcony on a spring day to enjoy the fresh air.

I slowly closed my eyes. As I slipped off to sleep, I had this question on my mind: "What year were we in? I wonder what year? I must ask the attendant . . ."

Off I went.

THE WINDOW IN ANKARA

The taxi stopped in front of Elfe's house. I gave the driver his money and slowly got out of the taxi. I raised my eyes a little and looked at the window above the entrance door.

The old doctor was there. He was sitting in his high-backed chair, looking out. He saw me. I saw a slight movement in his face, his mouth seemed to twitch a little, and he was looking at me with his pale blue eyes. The caretaker sitting next to him saw me too, and straightening up in her seat gave me a hello.

In two steps I had passed through the entrance and was inside.

"You're lost in thought," said Elfe.

"I'm thinking," I said.

"What are you thinking? Was your guy at the window?"

"He was . . . Elfe, do you know what I'm thinking? How does this old man's brain work, how does he comprehend the world, what is his memory like, I wonder?"

Elfe started to laugh.

"Couldn't you find anything else to worry about? I can't believe you," she said. "I don't know whether his brain is functioning or not, but it's clear that there's a big storm going on in his soul. He's flipped out! Flipped!"

"You think so?"

"What else could it be?" said Elfe.

"You think he's lost his mind?"

"He's sick. Very old. His mind is gone," said Elfe.

"Did you hear something from the caretaker?"

"No, I haven't heard anything. They don't take him outside anymore. He never leaves the house."

"Did he used to go out?"

"Of course he went out. He was even driving the car until recently."

I was astonished.

"Do you mean to tell me he was using a car at his age?"

"He was. He had a special parking place in front of the door."

"So that means something happened all of a sudden . . ."

"Well actually, these things don't happen all of a sudden, but I don't know," said Elfe. "Why are you thinking about this thing so much?"

"I don't know," I said. "People's minds interest me."

"The man's mind . . ."

"Maybe. The man's mind. That brain is like a broken machine now. It's giving out the wrong signals; maybe it's getting different images . . ."

"Who knows . . . ?"

"The brain and the soul are confused with one another. The control button that each of them uses every day isn't functioning. The button's out of service," I said.

"You think so?"

"Of course. He has desires and wishes. He expressed them with the letter that he came down and left in the middle of the night."

"With no censor."

"No censor," I said.

"Like an erotic film."

"Exactly the same," I said. "But the actor is very old."

"That's what makes the whole thing erotic," said Elfe. "Maybe if this doctor had been young and made such a proposal to you everything would have been very different . . ."

"Maybe he does think he's young."

"No, he knows what his situation is."

"How do you know that?"

"Because he wanted you to get Viagra."

"Right," I said. "He knows about Viagra."

"Of course he knows. After all, he's a pharmacist too."

"I wonder, do you think he ever used Viagra?"

"He did," said Elfe. "He used it years ago."

"Who knows?" I said. "Do you think he's senile?"

"If you ask me, he's senile . . . God, drop this, will you? I'm bored," said Elfe.

"Let's watch a movie."

"What do you have?"

"There's a Buñuel film, *Viridiana*."

"God, forget about that Spanish director now. That's a difficult film."

"Come on; let's go out for a walk."

"That's the best idea. Let's go out."

THE SEYR-I MARDIN

The view of the city from the Seyr-i Mardin was enchanting at night. Mardin Castle behind us was illuminated like a fireball, on the hill.

A soft light fell on all the courtyards and entrances, the minaret of the Şehidiye Mosque was like a tower of light streaming out of the earth, there were hundreds of lights burning around me. Mardin was like a shimmering jewel; all of a sudden it seemed to me like a giant spaceship, descending with all its lights blazing.

The city was like a spaceship sparkling with thousands of lights that had come down and landed on the hill across from us. It sat motionlessly there, very close to me, as though bringing me news that originated in the infinity of unknown worlds and altered time.

I observed this city, metamorphosed into a space ship, in admiration for a while from where I sat.

On the other side, Mesopotamia was dark, motionless, and silent. A night bird softly sang somewhere.

I heard the chair next to me being gently pulled back.

I turned and looked.

IZMIR

"The cannon's going to go off," said the stout hospital orderly at my bedside. His name was Mehdi, I had learned.

At that moment, "bang," the cannon went off. The tall windows of the ward, which went all the way up to the ceiling, shook.

"What cannon is that?"

"It's the *sahur*, the Ramazan morning meal," said Mehdi. "And you didn't sleep at all last night."

"I have a little pain. I drift off every once in a while."

I thought of something. "What day of Ramazan is today?"

"The seventeenth day," said Mehdi. "Thank God," he sighed a little.

"What month is this, Mehdi?"

"August," he said.

"What year are we in?"

"1949. Oh, you're just having some fun with me, I think."

"Take it easy, everybody's asleep in the ward," I said. "I'm not having fun or anything. These needles affect me. My mind keeps coming and going. That's why I asked. 1949."

"What medicine?" said Mehdi. "They're giving you a simple painkiller. It's like water."

"I don't know, maybe the fall affected me."

Mehdi was staring closely at my face.

"You seem like somebody from years in the future," he said. "The way you talk, the way you're so easygoing, the clothes you're wearing, the wristwatch . . . that single piece of rubber on the bottom of your shoe. These aren't things I've seen before. Your handbag . . . the way you have your hair . . ."

I giggled.

"I'm someone whose consciousness keeps coming and going," I said. "A patient with a fracture."

"The fracture will heal," said Mehdi.

I was silent.

Inside the ward, one could hear the sounds that people passing through a deep sleep produced, sounds that harmonized with the darkness and showed through the night that they were alive. A little sigh, a slight snore.

The windows were open. The hot air and the sounds of Izmir flowed in. So I'm in the year 1949. I have to understand this well, digest it. I mustn't allow the attendant to see my confusion.

In the year 1949 in Izmir, I broke my left ankle by falling head over heels in Varyant. A cast was put on in the Konak Maternity Hospital. I hope to God I don't wind up lame. That old x-ray machine downstairs where they took a picture of my ankle, that breakable glass syringe in the nurse's hand, the strange attendant's uniform Mehdi was wearing . . . Outside a lonely Izmir . . .

So I'm in the year 1949. Doctor Ayhan is treating me. He must be about twenty-six years old. I just figured it out in my head. In Izmir, a twenty-six-year-old doctor.

I opened my eyes a little. Mehdi had gone off, thinking I was asleep. He'd have a cigarette in the hall now. He did the same thing last night.

A little later, I saw the tip of the cigarette glowing like a firefly at the base of the wall.

I wondered when I would be able to walk.

I wanted to get out of here as quickly as possible and lose myself in old Izmir.

The doctor is twenty-six years old . . . I wonder how old I am.

A varicose vein in my leg caught my eye. I'm not all that young.

I thought of my purse. There might be a little money in my purse. I wanted to squeeze a little money into Mehdi's hand. My car keys might be there. My ID was always in a corner of the pink wallet.

"Where is my purse?"

I started to move around in my bed.

Mehdi was next to me.

"What's going on; did something happen?"

"My purse . . . When they brought me into the hospital I had my purse with me, didn't I?"

"Of course; it's here," said Mehdi. He picked up my old leopard print purse from down by my feet and held it out to me.

"Can we turn on a light?"

"The lights in the ward are out now. We can't turn them on, everyone's asleep," said the attendant. "It'll get light in a little while."

"Is it that late?"

I was surprised.

"It is," said Mehdi. "It's been a long time since the cannon went off."

"You're right."

I went through my purse in the darkness. I found a bunch of my keys. They were attached to a ring with an elephant on it. I got my change purse out. I had about 400 liras. They were right where I had put them.

I pulled out a twenty. I stuck it in Mehdi's pocket.

"That's completely unnecessary," said Mehdi. "What do I need that for, in the middle of the night . . ."

My car keys were in the right place. I couldn't find my ID card. I kept on rooting through my bag. My card case with the picture of Marilyn Monroe on it came into my hand.

I slowly opened the cover. The folded piece of paper was still in there.

I gently unfolded the paper. I read the first sentences in the light falling into the ward from outside.

. . . I am madly in love with you . . . I want to sleep with you . . .

THE SEYR-I MARDIN

The chair next to me was gently pulled back. I turned to look. Buñuel must have come.

Someone completely different was sitting in the chair. It was an elderly man. His dark skin was tanned by the sun. He had piercing, dark-colored eyes, and a nose like an eagle's beak. A thick beard. On his back was a shiny silver-colored cape that hung down. There was a young man standing perfectly erect behind his chair. His hair was long too, and he had strange clothes. He stood there completely motionless, staring at Mesopotamia stretching out before him.

Who was this man sitting in the chair? He had turned slightly toward me now.

He moved his thin lips. The golden rings set with stones on his fingers caught my attention. He was obviously strong, and didn't resemble anyone I had ever met before.

He lifted his head and looked into my eyes.

"I'm King Darius," he said. "Darius the First. I am the king here. I own all of this land."

I straightened up a little in my seat and greeted King Darius.

"I went through the ruins of Dara yesterday morning," I said. "I have some knowledge of you."

"Yes, the ruins of Dara," the king muttered. "Basically, nothing has remained on the face of the earth. A few tomb chambers, a small treasury they discovered, and the endless plains . . ."

"Yes," I said. "The excavations are still going on. A large portion of the ruins are closed to visitors. But still a very magnificent world, Your Majesty."

King Darius shook his head.

"I don't go there. I get bored with the excavations. Sometimes I come here and sit in the early evening. I have a sherbet and observe the world," he said. "My slave Alop is always at my side."

He turned around.

"Alop, order a rose sherbet for the lady; I'll have one too," he said.

Alop the slave bent down to the ground.

"At your service, sire."

Within two seconds he had vanished somewhere into the back of the Seyr-i Mardin.

A little later a waiter brought the rose sherbets on a shiny tray.

"Please," said King Darius.

I took the glass of sherbet from the tray.

To myself, I was saying, "Oh, if Buñuel would only come and see this man . . . it would be incredible! King Darius. This man, a sovereign from who knows how many thousands of years ago."

And the ancient man was sitting in the Seyr-i Mardin looking at Mesopotamia.

Alop the slave took his place behind the king again.

King Darius was silent and motionless as a statue, examining our surroundings with his gleaming eyes.

I took a sip from the rose sherbet. It was marvelous, made with lemon. As though it had been specially prepared for King Darius.

"Were you expecting someone?" King Darius asked.

"No," I said. "I like it here. I come and sit here when I have free time. The region, this silence, this extraordinary city behind us, in short everything here affects me."

King Darius slowly nodded.

"It's like that around here," he said. "It's a confined world here. Enchanting and mysterious. It doesn't easily let anyone who comes in go away."

He turned to Alop the slave.

"Fan us, my boy," he said.

Alop the slave pulled out a fan made of woven palm leaves

from within his cape. He started to wave the fan gently above our heads.

"Let's cool off a little," said King Darius. "The weather's heating up. It's hot here in the afternoon."

Alop the slave began to wave the fan a little more quickly now.

"Your Majesty," I said. "There's an air conditioner in my room. There might be a place with air conditioning in the back of the Seyr-i Mardin. If it gets too oppressive, we could go there."

The king was intrigued.

"What's an air conditioner?"

"It cools the air," I said. "You'd like it."

"I've never heard of it," said King Darius. He turned to the slave. "Have you heard of it, Alop?"

"I never have, sire," said Alop, bowing down to the ground.

"Let me invite you to my hotel," I said. "It's very close by. We'll turn on the air conditioner. You can cool off a little."

"Fine, let's go," said King Darius.

Alop pulled the king's chair back a little.

We started to go down the steps of the Seyr-i Mardin with the king in front and me behind.

In a short time we reached the street. There was no one to be seen in the noon heat.

We started to walk toward the hotel.

IZMIR

"The doctor will come soon to do his rounds, visiting the wards and the private rooms," said Mehdi. "The morning rounds."

I was going through my purse where I lay. I found my mirror with the handle decorated with multicolored stones that I had purchased from a street vendor on Istiklal Avenue. I took a look at my face. I looked without thinking about it, you know, and what I saw in the mirror was the face that I was used to seeing. I straightened out my hair a bit with my hand. My face was pale. It was clear that I was just beginning to struggle to get over the shock of falling in Varyant, breaking my ankle, and all of a sudden finding myself in 1949 Izmir.

"That's such a beautiful mirror!" said Mehdi the attendant. His eyes were fixed on the mirror I was holding, whose short handle was covered with sparkling red, green, and purple stones.

"It's a cheap little thing," I said.

"It doesn't seem like that at all," said Mehdi. "I've never seen a mirror like that before in all my life. It looks like it came out of a jewel box in a treasury."

I started to laugh.

"You should see what else . . ."

"It's really unusual. Enjoy using it," he said.

There had to be a lighter set with stones in my purse as well. I got it on Istiklal too, from the same man. I rooted through my purse and found it. There was a bunch of grapes made from purple stones on it. The leaf of the grapes was worked with deep green-colored stones. I had bought it for ten liras and tossed it in my bag.

"Take it," I said, and held it out to Mehdi. "You should have it. Take it as a keepsake."

Mehdi's eyes opened wide.

"You're giving me such a valuable thing . . ."

"Take it. I don't smoke."

The orderly took the lighter in his hand. He held it up to the light. He stared for a long time at the gleaming purple spray of grapes and the flashing sparkle of the green stones of the leaf.

"Thank you very much," he said. "This is the most valuable thing I own."

He took the lighter and put it in his pocket. Next to his cigarettes. The cheap Chinese lighter sold on the street had enchanted the hospital attendant in Izmir.

I put the mirror in the flap of my purse and leaned back on the pillow.

The women in the ward were talking with one another.

"What does that new one who came have?"

"Her ankle is broken, they say . . ."

Their voices came to my ear. They sounded like magpies. The windows of the ward, which extended all the way up to the ceiling, were open. The sounds of Izmir and the smell of the sea were drifting in.

The doctor was beside me.

"How are you?" he asked. "How did the night go?"

"I'm fine. I can't move my foot. No other problem."

"Good. Did they give you a painkiller?"

Mehdi jumped in. "They didn't. She didn't want it."

"Very good," said the doctor. "I'm getting you up on your feet today."

I looked at his pale blue eyes and seemingly impassive face. In the morning light the lines of his face seemed somehow more defined; he looked rested. His whole appearance was immaculate. It was clear that he was a very fastidious person.

"Walk in the hall a little with the nurse helping you," he said. "You'll use a cane."

Mehdi leapt up. "I'll get the cane."

"Tell Nurse Muazzez to be careful when she lifts the patient up."

The doctor continued around the ward. He had left me.

THE ZINCIRIYE HOTEL
MARDIN

I was walking quickly on the road in the Medrese Quarter. The hotel was across from the Zinciriye Medrese. King Darius was walking beside me with his silver-colored cape billowing out behind. Alop the slave followed us.

We reached the hotel. I took my card from the reception desk and headed toward the elevator.

"After you, King Darius."

"What is this? A little room?"

"It's an elevator. We'll go upstairs in this."

King Darius got on the elevator. Alop also reluctantly got on. I pushed the button. The door closed. The elevator started to ascend slowly.

King Darius asked in astonishment:

"What is this? Where are we going?"

"We've come up to the top floor, Your Majesty. So that we didn't have to tire ourselves coming up the stairs."

The elevator door opened.

We came out of the elevator, I in front, King Darius and Alop the slave behind. We started to walk down the stone hallway, the floor of which was covered with brightly colored carpets.

"It's unbelievable," said King Darius. "A room that goes up in the air. Like an ancient tomb. But airy."

Alop the slave was very excited. He kept blushing and then turning pale. In his confusion he dropped his fan on the floor.

"Calm down, Alop!" said King Darius.

Alop made a reverence down to the floor. He picked up the fan he had dropped without showing it to the king and stuck it in the folds of his cape.

"Is this where you're staying?"

"Here, King Darius."

I had come to my room. I opened the door with my card and entered.

King Darius asked:

"What's that thing you opened the door with?"

"A magnetic card. It's a key, King Darius."

"Fascinating," he said. We went into the room.

"Now I'll turn on the air conditioner for you. You'll cool off."

"It's nice in here," said King Darius.

Suddenly I realized that someone was reclining on the couch with the multicolored silk cushions. She was buried in the cushions, all curled up like a kitten.

It was Silvia Pinal. When she saw that we had come, she sat up a little. She was staring in curiosity at King Darius and Alop the slave.

"It seems you have a friend," said King Darius. He was looking very attentively at Silvia Pinal lying amidst the cushions.

Silvia Pinal straightened up and stood up now. She was barefoot, standing on the carpet. Her sandals decorated with jewels were lying next to the divan.

"Silvia Pinal," I said. "The famous star of the Mexican cinema. King Darius . . . king of this region, and his slave Alop."

King Darius took Silvia Pinal's hands in his two palms with an elegant gesture. Alop the slave greeted the blonde by bowing to the ground.

Silvia Pinal was confused.

"Are you coming from a film set?" she asked me.

"No. I came across the king at the Seyr-i Mardin. I brought him to my room to show him the air conditioner."

Silvia Pinal became more serious now. She bowed slightly toward King Darius. The king had still not let go of her hands.

Silvia Pinal's exotic perfume was wafting in waves across the room.

King Darius looked at each corner of the room, as though he were trying to get a good sense of this strange world he had entered.

"Please, sit down," said King Darius to Silvia Pinal.

He himself sat down next to Silvia Pinal on the couch with the cushions.

I pushed the button on the air conditioner. A cool breeze immediately started to blow through the room.

"Wind," said King Darius. "The winter wind. How strange."

"No, it's an air conditioner," I said.

Silvia Pinal said to me: "I hope I'm not disturbing you. I didn't know you had a guest. I came to talk a little about that letter."

"What letter?" asked King Darius.

"A letter that was delivered to me at midnight in the city of Ankara," I said. "A message."

The king shook his head from side to side.

"Was it something important?" he asked.

"It was," I said. "A letter that held a mirror up to a person's soul. Maybe it was that letter that brought us all together here."

"Interesting," said the king. "So a message . . . Does it have any connection with us?"

"No. It only concerns me."

"It makes one curious," said King Darius.

Silvia Pinal whispered, "I'd like to read it."

"I can't show that letter to everyone, Miss Pinal," I said.

"But you showed it to Buñuel."

I was silent.

King Darius inquired: "Who is Buñuel?"

"A very famous Spanish director. Miss Pinal is one of his stars," I said. "She's a star in his films."

"These are things I was completely unaware of," said King Darius. "So you're one of Buñuel's stars?"

"Yes," said Silvia Pinal, inclining her head slightly.

"A star . . . Are you in the sky?"

"No, I'm on the earth," said Silvia Pinal.

"But you're as beautiful as a star in the sky."

The Mexican actress blushed at this compliment from King Darius.

"Thank you," she said.

I pushed the bell.

"I'd like rose sherbet," I said. "With ice, please. Four glasses. Put some cinnamon on it."

THE WINDOW IN ANKARA

There was a stirring in the apartment building, a movement. There were sounds on the stairs.

Elfe said: "The artichoke seller is here, I think."

We opened the door. There were snatches of conversation, women's voices coming from upstairs. I saw the old doctor's caretaker running down the steps toward us.

She was very upset.

"What's the matter? Did something happen, Müveddet Hanım?" Elfe asked.

"The doctor," she said. "The doctor's run away. Did he come to you, by any chance?"

"He's not here. Nobody's come here," Elfe replied.

"He just quietly slipped out while we were putting out tea and biscuits in the salon! We have to find him!" said the woman. "He must have just gone out. He was in his pajamas. They'd notice him right away on the street."

Elfe and I became worried as well.

"Where could he go? An old man . . . ," I said.

"He ran away," said Müveddet. "I've had the feeling for days now that he was going to do something like this. And see, we let our guard slip. He just ran out the door."

"He must be somewhere right around here," said Elfe. "Did he have any money on him?"

"Not as far as I know. But he might have taken some," said the woman. "He's wanted to get away from here for a long time."

"Where does he want to go?" Elfe asked.

"Who knows . . . ? To places where he used to live, to worlds that he thinks still exist," said the woman. "He's always imagining them. And he's in love."

"In love?" I asked.

I suddenly turned bright red.

"Who's he in love with?"

"He didn't say at all," said Müveddet. "But he's in love. I know. He used to sit in front of the window and wait all day long for his lover to come. Maybe there is no such woman. She was just an illusion. But the doctor is in love with her, I know that.

WORLDS STILL THOUGHT TO EXIST

The old doctor was sitting at one of the garden tables in the Mado Café in Tunalı Hilmi. He had on a shirt and a pair of pants. His slippers didn't stand out and just seemed like a pair of sandals worn on this hot summer day.

He was staring at the crowds passing by with his pale blue eyes, as though he were actually combing one by one through the people passing in front of Mado. There was a gleam of happiness and excitement in his eyes. It had been a good while since he succeeded in escaping from the prison where he had been imprisoned in his pajamas.

He seemed entranced by the flood of people in front of him.

A little while later he changed his place and went to one of the tables farther back.

"Did the sun bother you, sir?" asked a waiter.

"Yes, it got too hot."

He was on the alert and realized that someone in the crowd might notice him. Now in the shadows of the café he leaned back, as though adrift in thought.

At the next table sat an old man with grey hair. He had come in leaning on his cane and picked a table in the back of the café.

The doctor turned to him at one point. "Where is Gülhane from here?" he asked.

"Which Gülhane?"

"Gülhane Hospital . . . Where is it, I wonder?"

"Really, I don't know," said the man at the next table. "Would you believe I've never heard of it? I just walk from the house and come here every day."

"I know Gülhane very well," said the old doctor. "But I just can't figure out where it is . . ."

"You'll find it, you will."

"I will. I'm determined to find it."

"Is it hard to find?" the old man at the next table asked. The hand reaching out for his coffee trembled slightly.

"It's not hard . . . but still it's hard. It's a strange thing," said the old doctor.

"My life passed there. It's where I spent day and night."

"In this city?"

"In this city. And someplace nearby too," said the doctor.

"Then you'll find it."

"I intend to find it."

"Very easy things get hard. One day. Out of the blue," said the grey-haired man.

"It's also as though hard things suddenly become easy," said the old doctor. "To do what the spirit wants."

"Is that so? I can't do it," said the grey-haired man. "It's not easy. I can't do anything."

"You got here . . ."

The grey-haired man moved slightly closer to the old doctor.

"You know what?" he said. "I'm running away. From the house, from my wife, I'm running away."

The old doctor laughed.

The man continued:

"I want to escape from the city too, actually. To go farther away . . . My wife scares me. 'You'll fall into the hands of a gang of beggars,' she says. 'Then you'll see.'"

"I don't think so. Nothing's going to happen," said the old doctor.

He leaned back again. He was carefully scrutinizing the crowd passing in front of Mado.

"Aren't you having anything to drink, sir?" said the old man.

"I forgot to bring money with me."

"Let me order you a coffee, if you permit."

"Thank you. I'll pay you back tomorrow."

The old doctor's black coffee arrived.

He took a sip of his coffee.

He surrendered himself into the arms of a world that was either familiar or completely unfamiliar.

KING DARIUS AND SILVIA PINAL

We were sipping our iced rose sherbets. The hotel room had become nice and cool.

King Darius got up from his place and walked around a bit on the carpet.

"The hot air is gone," he said. "This is something extraordinary. Inside the room here it's like an autumn day . . . Outside it's roasting from the heat."

Silvia Pinal stared closely at this unusual man. The slave was behind the king, trailing after him wherever he went, and when the king sat down, he stood in readiness at his side.

Silvia Pinal slowly asked King Darius:

"Who is this young man? He seems very attached to you."

"That's my slave. My slave Alop. And his father was my father's slave. He's a faithful slave."

"What does 'slave' mean?"

"A slave, you know," said King Darius. "Don't you know what a slave is? My man. I control his freedom. He does everything I want, loves me, and protects me. A helping spirit."

"Oh," said Silvia Pinal. "I understand. Like a lover. He's given over his freedom, his world to you."

King Darius started to laugh.

"He's not at all like a lover or anything like that. He's a slave, that's all. My slave. He's special, Alop. He has qualities that distinguish him from the other slaves."

"I'm His Majesty's slave," said Alop. "If he said to die, I would die."

King Darius said:

"Alop's been in the palace since he was a child. I brought him up. The queen likes Alop very much too."

Silvia Pinal asked:

"Where is the queen?"

King Darius said:

"The Queen has been ill for years. She's resting in the palace. With her companions. She doesn't come out in this sun, this heat."

"I understand, I hope she gets better," said Silvia Pinal.

She was sipping her sherbet.

King Darius said:

"So you're a star. A shining star. More beautiful than those bits of light in the sky. I'd like to have you as my guest in the palace. I'd like to show you my garden and my gemstones. Would you come?"

"I'd be honored," said Silvia Pinal.

"Then let's go to the palace," said King Darius.

He stood up.

The sunbeams shining in through the window were playing on his silver cape.

He turned to me. "We'll see one another again," he said. "I have many things to learn from you. I understand that."

"Wait, let me bring you down in the elevator," I said.

Silvia Pinal gathered her things. Alop the slave ran down the hall first.

I brought them downstairs.

A little later they were lost to the eye as they walked away in the Medrese Quarter.

I went up to the room.

Luis Buñuel was standing beside the window. He was all in black, and his slightly dark and sunken face seemed a little weary today.

"Don Luis!" I called out in greeting. "Where have you been? I wanted to introduce you to someone!"

"I was in the montage room," said Buñuel. "I worked all

night. I like to work with some of the details myself. Who were you going to introduce me to?"

"I was going to introduce you to King Darius and his slave Alop. They were around here a little while ago."

"King Darius . . . The emperor of Persia, Darius I?" asked Buñuel.

"That must be him," I said. "'I am the king of this place,' he said. He's a very interesting man. He came with his slave Alop to the Seyr-i Mardin. I met him there. He sits and looks at Mesopotamia there, once in a while . . ."

"So King Darius was here."

"Yes, a little while ago. You just missed him by a few minutes."

Suddenly I thought of something.

"Silvia Pinal came too!" I said. "She's interested in the letter the old doctor wrote me. King Darius took her to his palace. He said he would show her his gardens and collection of jewels."

Buñuel was looking at me incredulously.

"Silvia was here? She went to the palace with the king? These are astonishing things. Two people from completely different worlds, different times," said Buñuel. "Silvia Pinal, who won the Golden Palm at Cannes in 1961 for her starring role in *Viridiana,* and Emperor Darius, the king of these lands I don't know how many thousands of years ago."

"There's something about Mardin, Don Luis," I said. "Your being here is more intriguing than King Darius's being here. Isn't that true? King Darius is a part of this civilization, part of its past. A powerful emperor who ruled fifty million people in his day. Perhaps as important and powerful as Alexander the Great. For him to show up once in a while and gaze at Mesopotamia is perfectly normal. But for you to be here . . ."

Buñuel laughed.

"I'm after that letter and a story, you know," he said.

"That story is actually in Ankara," I said. "Behind that window above the street door."

"That's true," said Buñuel. "But you're in Mardin, you have the letter, and there are some things going on in your mind . . ."

"Are there? What's there in my mind?" I asked with real curiosity.

"There are," said Buñuel. "I feel it. You're creating a world. Something."

"Really?"

"Really."

WORLDS STILL THOUGHT TO EXIST

The doctor was still sitting at one of the tables farthest in the back of the Mado in Tunalı Hilmi. His elderly friend was beside him. He had moved from the neighboring table to the old doctor's table.

They were sitting together. The sun had declined and faded, and no longer reached back to the rear section of the pastry shop. Small decorated lamps made little spots of light in the interior. The café was preparing for evening. The customers seemed different. Now customers waiting for evening were sitting at the scattered tables. The makeup of the women seemed somehow out of the ordinary. Their rouge seemed darker, and their eyelashes extended out above their cheeks.

The old doctor was in the shadows. He looked at his friend sitting next to him.

"Do you remember everything, Mustafa Bey?" he asked.

"I remember everything," said Mustafa Bey. "I have my old world in the palm of my hand. I remember my childhood, adolescence, the day I got married, everything, all very well. The sudden anxiety I experienced before the wedding, then the years I spent with my wife, the springs and the falls, getting together with friends in the evening once in a while, winter days, the wind burning on my cheeks, I remember it all."

His eyes were fixed on the distance.

The old doctor said:

"I remember everything too. Izmir, long years ago; the horse trams in Istanbul; Izmir again; my years at the Konak Maternity Hospital; times when life was hard and others when it was easy; that quick affair I had with the nurse; my nights on duty, the endless freedom; the first years of being a doctor. It's as though they're all here, right in front of me.

"The nurse fell for me. It was like I saw the desire, the yearning in her eyes. I was very young. Later there were a lot of people in my life. Women . . ."

"Were there a lot of women?" asked Mustafa Bey.

"There were a lot of women," said the old doctor. "The way each one looked, her smell, her hair, I don't know, her desires, her needs were different. In the hospital where death is nearby, people get involved with each other more easily. If you see someone twist and die in bed, life seems to burst out of you at that very moment!"

Mustafa Bey said:

"I was an accountant. I just had my own little life. Not a lot of women. And I couldn't get to the ones I liked. Anyway, I had a wife."

The old doctor said:

"You're escaping from the house."

"Yes, I get out of there every day. I go back in the evening."

The doctor said:

"This morning was the first day I was able to escape from the house. And I have no intention of going back."

"Well, what are you going to do at night?"

"I don't know; I'll spend the night somewhere. In some dark spot, some shadow."

"Won't they look for you from home?"

"They won't find me," said the old doctor. "My wife is very old. The attendant won't be able to find me."

"Why did you run away, Doctor Bey?"

"I'm in love with someone," said the doctor. "There's a woman I'm crazy with desire for. Maybe I'll meet her. I'll find her. Our days on earth are numbered. I want to live the way I like from now on."

Mustafa was listening to what the doctor said, lost in the distance.

"So you're in love with someone," he said.

"Yes. I want her. I want her to be mine."

"How did you meet her?"

"First I just saw her," said the old doctor. "I followed her for a long time. She came to an apartment in the building where I live. The window . . . I always watched her from the window. When she came, when she left.

"Now finally I've been released from sitting behind the window," he said afterward. "I stretched out my hands. I found the world again. Just like my years in Izmir in the Konak Maternity Hospital."

"Wonderful," murmured Mustafa Bey. "How wonderful!"

"But I'm not as strong as I used to be," said the old doctor.

"It's like I'm imprisoned in this body. My arms, my legs . . . Everything's slow now. My back has no strength. But my spirit . . . My spirit is the same," he went on talking. "I'm like I was in old Izmir, in the Konak Maternity Hospital. Like when I was stroking Nurse Muazzez's breasts as we lay on the stretcher behind the door . . . in the darkness of the Izmir night. Listening to the moans coming from the wards, clumsily opening the nurse's legs, the sea breeze, the smell that came to my nose of a cigarette being smoked in the hallway."

Mustafa Bey listened to him with longing.

"Oh my God, it's evening again."

"Night," said the old doctor. "The nights were so colorful . . . Even in that little old hospital; the nights were so colorful . . . the scent of a woman in my nose . . . a woman's hair on my lip . . ."

"Sometimes I have accidents down there," said Mustafa Bey. "It just started. The other day it happened on the road. Going home. I went inside, and my pants were wet.

"'Senile!' my wife screamed at me. 'You senile thing, you wet yourself! Where were you off to this time?' she said."

He paused for a minute.

"I don't want to go home either," he said. "Tonight I won't go home either. The senile man won't go home tonight."

SILVIA PINAL
PRIVATE THOUGHTS

I'm mad at Buñuel. After that instant when we were close, he's suddenly like ice. He's distanced himself from me. But I felt that I affected him. He may be afraid that he's attracted to me. He became tougher on the set, started to be more exacting when we were filming scenes. As though he were doing it on purpose. To crush me.

"Silvia Pinal—once more."

"Silvia Pinal—speak with a stronger expression."

"Silvia Pinal—Silvia Pinal."

Then he goes off to his corner and puts on that invisible steel armor that envelops him. It's impossible to get to him then.

I'm sitting in a corner eating away at myself inside from nerves. He's off in his own world, with all the shutters down against the outside.

I came to Mardin in pursuit of him. I knew I would find him here. I went to that woman's hotel. The Zinciriye Hotel. It's an exotic world. They offer you sherbet scented with roses, couches with silk pillows. Buñuel had come and gone. I talked to the woman.

She's a strange one. She has some material in her hands that fascinates Buñuel. It's a love letter that an old man wrote to her filled with sex. A message of lust and desire.

She didn't show me the letter. She was uncomfortable. I felt it.

I went to her room again. This time she brought two people whom she said were King Darius and his slave Alop to the room. They were unusual men. Strange people. At first I thought they were actors. A little later when I realized they were genuine, I was really amazed.

The slave was a very innocent type. King Darius was intriguing. He had piercing eyes, like steel. A man who seemed like he held the whole world in the palm of his hand.

He was paying me compliments.

"Let me take you to my palace," he said.

"Okay," I said.

We left the woman alone by herself and went to the palace.

King Darius took me into an endless rose garden. Different colors, different varieties, on and on. There was an incredible scent of roses everywhere. It was marvelous. I felt dizzy, drunk. "Look," he said. "Those are the black roses of Halfeti. Did you ever see them before?"

There were black roses before me, like velvet. I was astonished.

"I've never seen these before," I said.

He gave the slave an order to pick a bouquet of roses for me. Black roses of Halfeti. A huge bouquet in my hand. King Darius beside me. He was asking me questions, making me tell him what I do. I told him that I act in films. He doesn't know what films are. He was a little interested. He has no idea what the cinema is.

He took a peerless diamond out from under his silver-colored cloak, and gave it to me.

"This is very valuable; why are you giving it to me?" I asked in surprise.

"To make you happy," he said. "It's just a piece of stone. But I know it makes you happy. Be happy. Because you made me happy. I'll have them take you back to the hotel. We'll get together tomorrow. I'll have them pick you up."

"That's not my hotel."

"Which hotel are you staying at?"

"In the Cercis Murat Mansion," I said.

"Let Alop take you there. Tomorrow morning I'll have you picked up," he said.

A bouquet of black, velvetlike Halfeti roses in my hand, a huge diamond as big as a walnut!

He kissed me on the lips. He called to the slave.

I went to the Cercis Murat with the slave.

I'm experiencing strange things. I threw myself down on the couch.

Are all these things real, or am I seeing hallucinations because of the hot weather?

I had them put the roses in a vase. I have to read that letter. I'm looking at the diamond, turning it over and over in my hand. It's real!

King Darius was going to go to his ill wife, probably. I sensed it.

The black roses were magnificent. No news from Buñuel.

The black roses of Halfeti had a wonderful scent.

1949 IZMIR
DR. AYHAN
PRIVATE THOUGHTS

I shaved and left the house. I walked quickly to the hospital. The wards were overflowing. There was the peace and quiet of Ramazan in the air. I think the assistant is fasting. Muazzez Hanım was ready, all dolled up, waiting for me to come. I knew it the second I saw her. She was thinking about last night. She flushed a little when she saw me. I have to be careful. Women are dangerous. And even though they're dangerous, they attract me. My poor mother is trying to get me to like some good girl. There are going to be guests tonight after the *iftar* evening meal, but I don't feel like seeing anyone. That woman I put in the ward . . . I've been thinking about her for a while. She's an unusual woman. As though she came from a different world, some other civilization. Everything about her is like that. Strange. The clothes she wears, her hair, her little pocketbook, the way she talks, everything is different. Her ankle is broken, and there's a cut next to it. I'm making her walk. She told me she had no place to go. But she's not poor. Now and then I catch her staring at my face and my eyes. As though she's looking for something in my face, in my eyes. As though she thinks I look like someone. Like she's looking for someone . . . yes, like she's looking for someone. Her eyes are like that. I was very meticulous about her ankle. I don't want her to wind up crippled. A nice lady. Stylish. Mysterious, actually. There's something about her, but I don't know what it is. I'm keeping away from her. As I do with all the patients. I keep a definite distance.

If I wanted to, I could have asked her a lot of things. I didn't ask anything. I don't think Muazzez Hanım likes her very much. Next to her she seems very provincial, very forced.

This woman is natural. I caught her looking at the ward carefully but in amazement one night. Those looks were like the looks of a child newly come into the world.

She interests me, this woman. I'm not going to release her yet. I wonder who she is. Where did she come from? What is it that she's after?

I'll figure it out.

THE ZINCIRIYE HOTEL
MARDIN

I stretched out on the bed. I turned the air conditioner that I had opened all the way for King Darius down a little.

I was full of thoughts.

I had met so many people in this room in this stone hotel, this unusual world with silk pillows and a couch, and at the Seyr-i Mardin, where I went every day. I was completely overwhelmed.

The director Luis Buñuel and his main star the blonde

beauty Silvia Pinal, the Persian king Darius and his slave Alop . . . They were so different from one another and came from such different worlds.

King Darius and Luis Buñuel. Two men with absolutely nothing in common. One of them a strange person who was a world-famous surrealist director, the virtual King of the Empire of Passion. He had won award upon award for his disturbing films, a Spaniard with a unique spirit of his own. The other a very powerful emperor who had ruled millions, had made those around him tremble, who had been the master of Babylon, Mesopotamia, and Persepolis. Alop the slave was a fine young man. It was obvious that he was very attached to the king.

Silvia Pinal was a master artiste who drew men to her like a magnet with her frozen blonde beauty and her aloofness. I was in the middle of this little confusion. I had come from Ankara to Mardin to relax and found myself in this new kind of life that seemed full of images that belonged to this place.

I was thinking about the old doctor and his midnight letter, which rested in my card case with the picture of Marilyn Monroe on it.

I am insanely in love with you . . . I want to go to bed with you . . . I want you to be mine . . .

As I lay there in my bed, I was full of curiosity at the same time.

What was King Darius doing now? What did Silvia Pinal experience in the king's palace? Why wasn't Luis Buñuel anywhere to be seen?

What was going on?

In fact there were things going on outside of me, and I wanted to become involved in them.

I wondered if I would ever see these people again.

They were all so colorful and so incredible. Maybe these people were some little trick my mind was playing on me.

Perhaps none of them really existed. Maybe it was all the Mardin Dream.

When I thought of this I felt myself to be very alone.

At that moment someone knocked softly on the door. I arose from my bed and slowly opened the door. Alop the slave was standing at the door.

"Excuse me," he said. "Did I wake you up?"

"No, I wasn't asleep."

"If you'd like, King Darius is expecting you at the palace. He said for me to bring you to him if you agreed."

"Wait, let me get ready," I said.

I took Alop into the entry area with the archway.

"Wait here for me."

I brushed my hair in front of the mirror. I freshened my makeup, and put on some deep red lipstick.

I looked at my watch. It was ten o'clock. A rather late hour to be invited to the palace. But I had gotten ready.

WORLDS STILL THOUGHT TO EXIST

"It's become pitch-black dark," said Mustafa Bey.

The two old men were sitting at a table in the rear section of the Mado Café in Tunalı.

"It's dark. My wife will be waiting. But I'm not going home," said Mustafa Bey.

"They'll be looking for me," said the old doctor.

"We'll go to some corner of a coffeehouse and spend the night there."

"Right, nobody would be able to find us in the corner of a coffeehouse."

Mustafa Bey asked:

"What's your name?"

"Ayhan."

"Right, you said it this afternoon. Let me go to the bathroom and then we'll leave."

"Let's go," said the doctor. "There's nobody left here."

The café had emptied out. A warm light rain had started to sprinkle outside.

Mustafa Bey returned.

"They were just about to put me in diapers," he said. "My wife's idea . . . because I'm wetting my pants."

The doctor said:

"Oh wait. Don't do that. The second you put diapers on, you're finished. You can't go outside. Then you're in their hands. You put on diapers, it's over!"

"Really? Well, I guess I was lucky to get away."

"What are you saying? I'm a doctor," said the old doctor. "I know about these things. Once you put on diapers, it's a different world."

"God forbid . . ."

The two old men left the café.

They were walking down the street side by side.

"Where's the coffeehouse?" asked Mustafa Bey.

"We'll find one."

"Where is there one, some kind of okay place?"

"There are a lot in Kızılay. But I don't know which way Kızılay is."

"Cebeci," said Mustafa Bey. "There was a coffeehouse I used to go to in Cebeci that was open until the morning."

"If we just find our way to Cebeci," said the old doctor. "Cebeci, Cebeci, which way is it from here? I think maybe you go from over there . . ."

"No, no, it's from here," said Mustafa Bey.

The two men seemed as though they were in a labyrinth.

"If we turn there . . ."

The old doctor responded:

"We'll get lost. It could be dangerous. I'm going to ask someone the way."

He asked a young man who was passing by:

"Which way is Cebeci?"

"It'll be hard for you to get there from here."

"Why?"

"You have to go to Kızılay and take something."

"I understand."

The old doctor turned to Mustafa Bey.

"Cebeci's difficult," he said. "It's not going to be easy for us to make it to Cebeci. We'll have to find a coffeehouse somewhere else . . ."

"Kurtuluş," said Mustafa Bey. "There's a coffeehouse in Kurtuluş."

"Kurtuluş . . . how can we get to Kurtuluş?"

"I have no idea . . ."

"Let's spend the night someplace nearby. That's the easiest," said the old doctor.

The nighttime labyrinth of the city had enveloped them.

"Cebeci, Kurtuluş, Kızılay," muttered the old doctor. "I used to walk there. Now in this night it's like each one is a separate country."

"Really," said Mustafa Bey. "If we turn onto that road . . . I think it goes to Cebeci."

"I don't think that goes to Cebeci. Let's walk this way."

"There's some old-time music playing. Do you hear it, Doctor?"

"I do," said the doctor. "It's an old song. Where is it coming from?"

"The music is coming from the open window in the first floor of that apartment building."

"Where's the door of the building?"

"It's that green iron door."

"Let's go see what's up."

The two old men, pushing the iron door, entered into the dim entryway of the building.

"Something smells bad here," Mustafa noticed.

"It's a cat smell. Let's go upstairs," the doctor replied.

The automatic light went on. The faint light illuminated

the faded yellow walls and black steps of an old dilapidated Ankara apartment building. They started to climb the stairs. There was a door on the first floor. The sound of music came from there.

"It's an old 78," said the doctor.

There was an overweight woman past her prime standing at the door.

"Please," she said. "Come inside."

"What is this place?" asked Mustafa Bey. "We don't want to disturb you."

"Come in, come in," said the woman. "Come inside. This is a house for the Night People."

KING DARIUS AND THE MARDIN NIGHT

I had arrived with Alop the slave at the ruins of Dara. The ruins looked mysterious and eerie in the moonlight.

A dog barked in the distance. The air had grown cool. We slowly entered the ruins of Dara.

"There may be holes," I said to Alop the slave. "My eyes don't see well in the darkness. Is this the king's palace? It's pitch-black here, these are ancient ruins . . . thousands of years old. A wild animal could be hiding in those mausoleums over there."

I was anxious. King Darius could not possibly be around here. We were walking over the lifeless stones of a world that had lived and died. It was dark everywhere. I could make out the tall mausoleums on either side in the moonlight.

"Here we are," said Alop the slave. "Can you climb up there?"

He respectfully held out his hand to me.

"But there's a hole there. Terrifying! This is a tomb!" I cried out.

"No, it's not. Don't be afraid. Trust me," said Alop the slave.

I took the hand he held out to me. He gently pulled me up.

"Step on that stone."

I stepped on it. We moved a few paces forward in the darkness.

Alop touched the earthen wall.

All of a sudden we entered a world illuminated with thousands of torches burning on its walls. Delicate flames played on the tops of the walls. A deep red carpet covered the floor of the hallway we were walking in.

"Very beautiful!" I murmured. "A world of enchantment!"

"King Darius's world!" said Alop. "We're here now."

King Darius was standing at the end of the hallway.

"Please," he said. "I trust you weren't frightened as you were coming in. The ruins are a little off-putting in the darkness."

"It's very beautiful here!" I said.

I was looking around in admiration.

"Come," said King Darius. "Let's sit on the terrace. Let's look at Mardin. There's a full moon tonight. I thought you might like it."

We went out onto a marble terrace. Mardin spread out in front of us like an island of light.

"I had them extinguish the torches," said King Darius. "So that you could see the city better in the darkness."

"It's an enchanting view," I said. "I can't see this from my hotel."

"This is a very high and special place," said King Darius.

We sat down on stone seats. Alop brought cushions to us.

"Let's look at Mardin," said King Darius.

"Let's look at Mardin," I said.

For a while I looked at the display of light before me.

"It's so unusual," I murmured. "The whole area and Mesopotamia are dark at night, but Mardin is so bright. As though . . . as though Mardin was like a space ship," I said. "A space ship landed on top of a hill . . . All its lights are on, and I can see its little portholes . . ."

"What did you say?" asked King Darius.

"Mardin looks like a space ship."

"And what's that?"

"Nothing, actually. There may not really be anything like that. But sometimes on starry nights you can see a ship that comes from space, filled with other creatures . . . It looks like that."

King Darius asked with curiosity, "Have you ever seen a ship like that? A space ship . . . a heavenly ship?"

"I never have," I said. "Maybe there really are no space ships. It's just an idea. Some people believe they exist . . ."

King Darius was listening to me attentively.

"How beautiful," he said. "Magical . . . A space ship. People inside it."

"People who came from another planet," I said.

"Where did they come from?" asked the king.

"From another star."

"Oh, how beautiful . . . When you said 'star' I remembered something. I entertained Miss Silvia Pinal here on this terrace tonight as well. She also talked to me about completely different worlds. About film sets, scenarios, film festivals . . . She talked about a city called Venice where the streets are made of water. It's like a fairy tale, isn't it?"

"She probably told you about the Venice Film Festival," I said. "The film *Viridiana*, in which she played the lead role, won the Golden Palm award in 1961 at the Cannes Film Festival. Buñuel has won a lot of awards at the Venice Film Festival. He won the Golden Lion with *Belle de Jour*."

"Yes, things like that," said King Darius. "I just remembered Venice. A magic city. Now you're telling me about a space ship."

He called Alop the slave, and said something into his ear.

At this juncture two beautiful girls, who I guessed were slaves, brought us fruit and sherbet.

"This is mulberry juice!" I said.

"Yes, mulberry juice," said King Darius.

"Whenever I go down to Kadiköy Square in Istanbul, I always have them squeeze a glass of this for me at the place that sells fruit juice there and I drink it," I said. "Mulberry juice . . . In an instant it reminded me of Istanbul, the crowds in the market square in Kadiköy, the bookstores I went in and out of, the famous sweet shop on the corner, and the coffee cups with roses on them that I got from Ce-zi-ne. I recalled a part of my life that I enjoyed living so much, the bookstores there selling old books, the little fountain inside the Yanyalı Fehmi Restaurant on the corner down below, the home cooking on display in the windows, the fish shops, and the enormous polished apples in the greengrocers."

Mardin in front of me was like a flying saucer. I couldn't take my eyes off this mass of light.

King Darius said:

"What beautiful things you said. A world . . . Kadiköy, the market square."

Alop the slave came with a huge bouquet of perfectly black roses in his hand. King Darius took the roses and gave them to me.

"These are the black roses of Halfeti," he said. "They don't grow anywhere else."

I looked at the roses.

They were like velvet. So beautiful.

The king took a purple jewel out from the silver folds of his cape. It was transparent, as large as a chicken egg. He held it out to me.

"This is yours," he said. "In its depths, you'll be able to see those worlds and the space ship you described to me anytime you want."

I took the stone from his hand in astonishment. "What is this?"

"It's a seer stone," said the king.

"What does 'seer stone' mean?"

"It's like a crystal ball, a stone that's connected to your heart and mind. You can see the things you want and desire in this stone."

"How fascinating!" I said. "Are the images just for me?"

The king thought for a minute.

"Yes," he said. "You could say that they're just for you, private images. You can see whatever you want!"

"Will I see real things?"

"Your thoughts, your dreams," said the king. "The seer stone . . . When a person has this he'll never be bored."

"Like television," I murmured.

"What's that?" asked King Darius.

"There's a thing called television," I said. "Images, conversations, discussions, news . . . it shows them. But it's not mysterious like the seer stone. In fact, television's become a little boring. It has one-sided programs. And the programs are awful. There are serials . . ."

"Sounds interesting," said King Darius. "Could we get one of them here?"

"We can get one right away tomorrow," I said. "When the shops open in the morning. We'll get you a large screen LCD for here."

"Wonderful!" said King Darius.

"Look at the seer stone tonight and try it out. Tomorrow we'll go to the shops together."

My visit was over.

Thanking King Darius, I stood up. Alop the slave accompanied me down the red-carpeted corridor and brought me out from the palace.

It was pitch-dark outside. We walked through the ruins and emerged outside the remains of Dara.

Alop the slave was carrying the black roses in his hand. I had the seer stone. I gripped it tightly, excited.

A little later we came to the hotel. I entered the brightly lit stone lobby. I took the roses from the slave. We said goodbye and I went up to my room.

When I put the card in the slot, I found the room lit up. My bed had been turned down. I put the black roses in a glass vase I found on the tabletop. They were incomparably beautiful. It was like there was a Hollywood star wearing a black velvet gown in the room now. The roses were that beautiful, their scent was that beautiful, that overpowering. I sat on my bed. I started to turn the seer stone over and over in my hand.

WORLDS STILL THOUGHT TO EXIST (ŞEVKI BEY GETTING FED UP)

The short, plump woman was wandering around in the room, wearing a black jersey skirt with ruffles and a sleeveless blouse the color of moonlight. She had short hair with tight curls that made one think of a bird's nest, and fuzzy slippers on her feet. Occasionally she patted the silk cushions on the couch or straightened the edges of the lace doilies on the side tables in the room. The gramophone in the corner was playing a 78 rpm record, and the voice of a woman from the distant past filled the room with waves of sound.

In this room that reminded one of an old-fashioned reception room for guests, there were velvet armchairs with wooden arms, frosted glass sconces in the shape of grape bunches, dark green walls, and in the corner, an old varnished console table. Everything was perfectly arranged, as though it had been this way for years and would continue to be forever. In the crystal candy bowl on the low table in the middle were a few pieces of Turkish delight with coconut on top. This was the room of an aged aunt or a grandmother. Everything was a little old and worn here, and it gave the room a unique feeling and loveliness. There was an almanac calendar hung on the wall next to the door. The only painting decorating the walls was the painting of a grave-looking pasha. The pasha seemed to be continuously surveying the room with his close-set eyes and bristling moustache . . . The old doctor and Mustafa Bey came into the room.

The woman again spoke:

"Come in, make yourself comfortable. Should I turn down the gramophone a little? Ephtalia the Mermaid is singing."

"Oh, how wonderful!" said the doctor. "Don't turn it down. It's wonderful."

The two old men who had entered this Night Salon didn't feel in the least like strangers. They sat down in armchairs.

"Isn't there anyone else?" Mustafa Bey asked.

The woman said:

"They're still on the way. The night's still young."

The old doctor said:

"My house is like this. Actually it looks a lot like it. Almost the same side tables."

Mustafa Bey said:

"My salon is more or less the same. My wife keeps it shut up when we don't have guests. We put the television somewhere else."

"I had them put the television in the salon," said the doctor. "But I don't watch it very much. My real television is the window. When the morning comes, I open the two sides of the curtains and sit down in front of it. Life outside . . ."

"Well, we're in life now," said Mustafa Bey. "And night life at that."

The old telephone in the corner with a doily over it rang.

"Hello? Şevki Bey, how are you? I'm expecting you. I've been worried. You're never this late. Come on over . . ."

She listened to the voice coming from the other end of the receiver for a while.

"You don't say! How did it happen? I can't believe it. Oh my God! What are we going to do now?"

The voice on the other end was quickly relating something.

The woman nodded her head in disappointment.

"Oh, Şevki Bey, oh! But still give it a try. Come like that.

There are friends here. We're waiting for you."

She put down the telephone.

She turned to the old doctor and Mustafa Bey, who were sitting side by side.

"What a shame!" she said. "Just look at the way of the world. Life is pitiless. Şevki Bey . . . he's old, a former civil servant. He comes here every night and stays for a while, then I put him in a taxi downstairs. He goes home. He found happiness here in his old age. Freedom, you know . . ."

"What happened to him?" asked the old doctor with curiosity.

"They diapered him," said the woman. "They diapered him just early this evening. They put his pajamas on. He can't go outside anymore. With some kind of monster as a caretaker . . . The poor man. He was so refined. A complete gentleman. Now he's become an infirm old man with one foot in senile land."

After pausing a minute, she added, "He may not be able to leave the house now."

"This is a terrible thing!" shouted Mustafa Bey. "Why did they diaper him?"

The doctor muttered:

"A shame! He must have been wetting himself. I told you. When you get diapered a different world begins . . ."

"Oooh! I don't even want to think of it."

The blonde woman said:

"Now don't even think of those things here. Just relax."

A sound came from the staircase. The woman opened the door.

"Come in, Hıfzi Bey," she said. "Welcome."

An old man with a walking stick entered.

"I managed to get away again tonight," said the newcomer. "I'm in seventh heaven. Let me sit down there." He went over to the armchair in the corner and sat down.

"Let me make you all some coffee," said the woman.

She disappeared in the direction of the kitchen. The doctor looked at the newcomer.

Mustafa Bey inquired:

"Are you coming from home?"

"From home, from home," said the man. "It was hard to get out. My wife, my daughters, the son-in-law, they were all in the house. I slipped out tonight while the son-in-law was watching the match . . . How about you?"

"We slipped out of the house too," said the doctor.

"And we have no intention of going back," said Mustafa Bey.

"What did you used to do?"

"I was a military doctor. I'm retired. Mustafa Bey here was an accountant."

"I was an independent accountant," said Mustafa Bey.

"Whereabouts do you live?"

The doctor said:

"Well, it's close by, but I just can't place where right now. When you cross the avenue . . ."

"My house is in a confusing place too," said Hıfzi Bey. "I come by taxi every night. A taxi from the stand at the corner . . . he brings me."

"We're just new," said the doctor. "We walked here. We were going to go to Kızılay. To Cebeci, but we couldn't figure it out."

"Oh, it's really difficult around there," said Hıfzi Bey. "I haven't been there for years. It's a mess."

"You're right."

The woman brought in the coffee on a shiny tray.

She put the coffees one by one on the coffee table, in front of the old men.

The doctor leaned over and picked up his cup of coffee. He took a sip.

"Blessings to your hands. It's very good," he said.

"I hope you enjoy it," she said.

"I have a girlfriend," said the doctor. He leaned back in his armchair.

The two men looked at him enviously. Hıfzi Bey asked in curiosity: "Is she young?"

"Young and beautiful," said the doctor.

"How do you manage? I mean, how . . . to keep her around . . . ?"

"Viagra," said the doctor.

There was a silence in the room.

"Really?" asked Hıfzi Bey. "Why don't you tell us about it?"

"I've only been able to give her a letter so far."

"But even that is a great achievement," said Mustafa Bey. "Were you able to write it yourself?"

"I wrote the whole thing."

"How did you get it to her? It's not easy. You've done the most difficult part."

"I left the letter in a mailbox."

"Oh, but did she get the letter? Did she read it?" said Hıfzi Bey.

"She found it and read it. Because I told her on the phone where I had left it."

"That's talent for you!" said Mustafa Bey. "To be able to do that . . ."

"Yes. Luck helped. I gave her my own cell phone number."

"Was there a reply?"

"Not yet. She's thinking it over."

Mustafa Bey asked:

"Where's your cell phone?"

"I forgot it at home when I was leaving. But anyway, I would have turned it off and not used it."

"You're right; they find us from the cell phones."

Hıfzi Bey said:

"If I don't return, I don't think anybody would even care. But, you know, old habits. I get in my own bed every night. My body's used to it . . ."

The old men were continuing their conversation as they drank their coffees.

Noises came from the staircase. The woman went outside.

An old man in pajamas came into the room.

"I managed to escape," he said. "The attendant got involved talking to his girlfriend. He went out into the hall to light up a cigarette. I rushed out and came here. I'm wearing a diaper."

"No problem!" the people in the room all shouted with one voice.

"Oh, let me sit down over there!"

Şevki Bey flung himself down in the nearest chair. He crossed his legs.

"Let me bring you a coffee too, Şevki Bey," said the woman. "I'm so happy you were able to come."

The woman disappeared into the back, where the kitchen was.

Turning to Şevki Bey, Hıfzi Bey said:

"Brother, this is a big success. You've pulled off a great thing. Being able to slip out of your bed and come over here after they put you in diapers . . . like coming back to life. And with that gorilla of an attendant at your throat."

"Like a prison guard," said Şevki Bey. "They just hired him. He's like a wrestler. Doesn't care about anything, no feelings. He worked in a center for old people before this. He always has a cell phone in his hand, talking to his girlfriend. His name is Mahmut. He smokes a pack of cigarettes a day.

"'Son, look, you're still young. You should value that. Don't smoke that poison,' I say. 'Don't worry, Pop,' he says."

"Could you imagine that?" the doctor remarked. "Well, never mind, forget about all that now. Let's enjoy the night."

Ephtalia the Mermaid was passing from one song to another on the 78.

The night had settled down on the city. Lights were turned on where they should be, turned out where they should be too.

Night was at its peak now. It floated in waves above the city like a printed black cloth.

THE BLACK ROSES OF HALFETI

I was stretched out on the bed in my room in the Zinciriye Hotel, amid the silk pillows. I gazed around at the high ceiling and the bare stone walls.

The black roses of Halfeti were in a glass vase. Once put in water, they opened even more and gave off an incredible scent. My eyes rested on them.

King Darius . . . The magnificent and eerie ruins of Dara . . . Mardin, which looked like a space ship from the terrace of the palace . . . These were all mysterious things . . . Suddenly I noticed that the black roses had trembled slightly. I stared closely at them.

The black velvet Halfeti roses were moving. What I was witnessing was like a chick forcing its shell as it emerges from the egg, as it struggles to free itself from the thin envelope that surrounds it and come out into the world.

An action, an effort . . . The black roses seemed to converge for a moment, and from within them emerged a woman. She then managed to extract herself from the bouquet of roses, and now stood in the center of the room in a black velvet gown. She straightened the blonde hair that fell onto her shoulders, and ran her tongue lightly over her gleaming red lips. She was very beautiful. I stared at her in amazement. She had pure white skin and a perfect body in her tight velvet gown.

"Who are you?" I asked. She must be an artist, and seemed to radiate some kind of luminescence.

"Who are you?

"I'm the Dream Woman," she said.

"The Dream Woman . . ."

"Yes, the Dream Woman. The woman in men's dreams!"

"I thought you were a Hollywood star."

"No, no," said the woman. "I'm just the Dream Woman. The woman who embellishes a man's illusions, whom he wants to conquer, whose existence he is aware of but whom he usually cannot attain."

"How very interesting," I said. "What were you doing in the middle of the black roses?"

"I came out into the world from there tonight," she said. "Black velvet roses, they're so beautiful . . ."

She looked at the black velvet roses in the vase behind her.

"What do you do, how do you appear to men?" I asked curiously. "Do they imagine you?"

"They imagine me, of course," said the woman.

She sat down on the edge of the bed.

"I adorn their dreams. I enter their dreams," said the woman. "I wander about in their dreams; I make love to them."

"It's an incredible thing," I said. "Does every man see you?"

"Every man," she said. "They all see me and desire me."

I was thinking.

"Did you go into King Darius's dreams?" I asked.

She laughed in a sexy way.

"I was thinking about going into his dreams tonight," she said. "Who knows how intriguing his dreams might be? He's a very ancient king. I'll go into his dreams in a little while."

"There's Luis Buñuel, a famous Spanish director. You probably have gone into his dreams!"

"Oh, I've been in the dreams of all the directors," said the woman. "That's my job. I went into the dreams of the famous French director Roger Vadim years ago; when he woke up he made stars out of Brigitte Bardot, Annette Stroyberg, and Catherine Deneuve, one after the other."

"My goodness," I murmured. "Well, let's say you just inspired him."

She smiled a little.

"Maybe," she said.

"Do you always appear in the dreams of famous, powerful men?"

"No, no!" said the Dream Woman. "I also enter the dreams of the old and the poor."

"The poor . . ."

"Yes, I also go into the dreams of civil servants, laborers, people who get by on a little. They're astonished to see me in their dreams. They invite me to sit in the best places, they're all over me, the man doesn't want to wake up. Sometimes I have a difficult time getting out of those dreams," she said.

What she said was mesmerizing.

"The dreams of men who are used to beautiful women are much duller," said the woman. "I go into the dream, he sees me and gives me a once-over. Then he either picks up on me or forgets about it, since he's used to women like me. He doesn't bother with me," she said. "Sometimes I come out of those dreams feeling hurt."

"And what about a middle-class person's dream?" I asked.

"Well, that's incredible! I've experienced unbelievable things in this kind of dream. The man whose dream I go into worships me."

She stopped for a minute.

"I have many memories," she said. "I'll tell you . . . I went into the dream of an old man named Hıfzi the other night in Ankara—just by chance. All of a sudden! The man was amazing. Old. It was as though he's living between two worlds. Hıfzi Bey . . . I'll never forget him. I'm thinking of going into his dream again. Just out of the blue again!

"The guy got younger in the dream, as though he were resurrected. It was something strange. I just went into his dream. I don't know him, never met him.

"He wrapped himself around me. It was as though he had thrown off the weight of years in an instant. He didn't want to let me go.

"'Please come again!' he said. 'Let's be together.' There's a group. They meet in the Night People's house in Ankara. A group of old people who are on the brink of losing their memory. He told me about it, an old-fashioned salon. They cling to life there."

She paused briefly.

"These things that Hıfzi Bey said really interested me," she said. "I'm going to go into his dreams again. Hıfzi Aygün. He gave me his name. 'Make sure you don't mess everything up,' he said. He's retired from some place. I forget it now, but the world he described that night was incredible."

She stood up.

She was fixing herself up now.

"It's time," she said. "I'll go into a dream."

She pulled out a little cell phone from within the folds of her black velvet gown.

"There's a message," she said.

She pushed a button and started to read.

"Are you going to enter the dreams of King Darius?"

The woman shook her head.

"No, no," she said. "A different dream has been set up for tonight. Dr. Ayhan. An old man from Hıfzi Bey's group. They're in the same salon now. You know, the one I just told you about."

I was intrigued.

"A military doctor?"

The woman was taken aback.

"Yes," she said. "A retired military doctor. But do you know him?"

"I sort of know him."

"Well, I'm going into his dream now. The message came."

She fixed her hair, spread some gloss on her lips. She concealed her little black purse in the skirts of her gown.

"I'm going now," she said. "I'll come again."

"Stop by when you come out of the dream," I said.

"You'll be asleep . . . I don't want to wake you up."

"No, no, I won't sleep," I said. "I'll wait for you."

"Okay, say goodbye to me for now," said the woman.

She disappeared somewhere behind the roses.

I was full of odd feelings. What the Dream Woman had told me had fascinated me.

She could go in and out of every kind of brain. This was the most important thing a woman could want, as far as I was concerned.

I didn't know how influential she was. After all, she was, in the end, an illusion. But I could learn a lot of things from her.

So the old doctor was meeting up with his friends in the Night People's house. He must have escaped from home.

DR. AYHAN'S DREAM GATE

I was moving quickly down a narrow passageway. Along the sides old women and men and one or two young people were gathered waiting. It was a place like the jetway leading onto a plane; it wobbled slightly when I walked. I didn't know exactly where I was going, but it was as though some force were pushing me from behind or pulling from in front.

I asked an old woman waiting on the side, "Where is this? What are you waiting for here?"

"The apron," said the woman. "It's the entryway to dreams. We're mainly old mothers and fathers here. We're waiting to get into dreams. You know, mothers and fathers don't often appear in dreams."

"I know," I murmured.

"So you're old mothers and fathers . . ."

"Most of us are," said the woman. "We're waiting for a message to go into the dreams."

"Whose dream would you go into?"

"I'm going into my daughter's dream," said the old woman. "I've been waiting in line for a week. My daughter is ill. If she sees me in her dream, she'll pull herself together and improve a little. But it's taking a long time, as you see. The line is very crowded, and the visiting period is short. And I'm just waiting here."

"Inshallah, your turn will come soon," I said.

I was running forward in the passageway now. Around me, waiting to enter dreams, were former mothers and fathers, a few children, a handsome young man I imagined to be an old lover, and a few men wearing hats. A strange, silent crowd of people . . .

As I passed by, I inquired of a young man with green eyes whose hair was combed back, "Are you in the line for dreams?"

"Yes," he said.

"Whose dream are you going to go into?"

"I'm a former fiancé," he said. "Former fiancé . . . a fiancé who left while still in love. The ring was cast off because of the mother-in-law. She's in love with me. I'm waiting my turn. I'll get into her dream and deliver my message."

I was touched by what I heard.

"Why don't you just see her yourself and talk? Wouldn't that be easier?" I asked.

"No," said the young man. "How can that possibly be? Nothing is as influential as a dream. A dream can influence someone much more than real truths. Think about that."

I thought about it as I rushed forward. What the former fiancé said was right.

A dream . . .

I came to a doorway. This was a place like a pilot's cockpit. It was covered with a dark-colored velvet curtain.

The young woman standing by the door, whom I understood to be on duty, said, "You will go in a little while. Move quietly. Don't talk too much. Gentle movements. Don't stay too long. You can go in when the red light goes on."

"Fine," I said. I fixed my collar, straightened my skirt. I had on the new patent leather shoes I had purchased from Kemal Tanca. They were gladiator shoes that wrapped around the foot like a cage, with thin heels. I had to be careful not to get caught anywhere. I wondered where I was going.

"Whose dream?" I asked the girl on duty.

She looked at the list hanging on the wall.

"Dr. Ayhan Ozer's dream. It's the second time you've been called. You didn't come the first time. That's why we're taking you in a hurry."

"I didn't know I'd been called the first time," I said.

"No problem," said the woman. She pulled the curtain aside. "Go in there," she said. "The light is on."

I looked, and there was a red light burning above the door of the cockpit. I slowly stepped in through the opening in the curtain.

It was a half-dark world. Dim. A little dreary.

I went inside. It was a fairly large bedroom. The only bed in the room was standing against the opposite wall, covered with a silk quilt. The dark beige curtains were drawn. Next to the bed was a night table with a pitcher of water for the night and a glass on it. Only the little light on the table was lit. Its parchment shade was rather old; it gave an apricot-tinted light to the room.

The doctor was in the bed. He was sitting there, resting back on two pillows.

The Dream Woman in her black velvet gown was sitting at the foot of the bed. When she saw me come in she waved her hand.

"Come, come . . . he wants you in his dream. He didn't have any reaction to me at all," she said.

The old doctor saw me. He straightened up a little then.

"Welcome," he said. He held out his hand to me.

I reached out and shook his thin, bony hand.

"Well, let me go then," said the Dream Woman.

"Don't leave, stay a while," I said. "Is the doctor ill? Why is he lying in bed?"

"He's sick," said the Dream Woman. "His mind is confused. He confuses everything."

The doctor was silent. He was staring directly at me.

"My letter," he said. "Did you get my letter?"

"I did," I said.

At that moment the bedroom door opened. His attendant, Müveddet, came inside.

"Doctor Bey, what's going on? Are you seeing ghosts?" she asked.

"I'm not seeing ghosts. It's all real. You go outside," said the doctor.

"I came to give you your medicine."

Müveddet filled a glass with water and gave the doctor his medicine. I realized that she didn't see us.

"Now just lie down nicely there, Doctor Bey," she said. "Close your eyes and go to sleep. There's still a long time till morning."

She went outside.

The doctor turned to me.

"I've fallen into their hands," he said. "She's an even simpler woman than the character Solfasol. Snoopy. A gossip . . ."

He was quiet for a minute.

"I want to say something," he said. "There's a home for Night People in Tunalı Hilmi Avenue. Come there. A woman runs it. It's a proper, well-run place. I'm there now."

"I'll try to find it," I said.

"I'm expecting you there, I'm expecting you!" said the doctor.

He was excited.

The Dream Woman gave me a little signal.

"The light is blinking. Come on, we're leaving," she said.

The two of us left together through the cockpit doorway with the dark grey velvet curtain.

She looked at my feet.

"Your shoes are very beautiful!" she said. "That old man is in love with you. What are you going to do?"

"I really don't know," I said.

"It's hard."

"Yes."

The curtain had closed behind us. I felt like I had been suddenly picked up and tossed down into the middle of silk pillows.

It must be nearly morning. I looked for the Dream Woman, but she was nowhere to be seen. The sound of the call to prayer filled my room. The call was coming from the Şehidiye Mosque.

What I had seen must surely have been a dream. But I couldn't actually figure out whether it was a dream or not. It seemed real. I had lived it. Slowly I buried my head in the pillow and fell into a deep sleep.

THE BLACK ROSES OF HALFETI

I was slowly opening my eyes. I felt the presence of someone else in my room. I opened my eyes and looked around.

The Dream Woman was sitting at the foot of my bed.

"Oh, I woke you up," she said. "Forgive me. I tried not to make any noise, but you woke up. Those latticework shoes of yours with the thin straps are really nice. There are tiny little stones on them . . ."

"Take them for yourself," I said. "You like them. Take them"

"No," said the Dream Woman. "They look so chic on you. I'll get the same ones . . . Do you know, these shoes would go well in dreams?"

"I can imagine," I said. "Every detail you see in a dream is important."

"Yes," she said. "Even the smallest detail seen in a dream is important."

"Did we go into the old doctor's dream last night?" I asked.

"Was he a doctor? Yes, of course we did," she said.

"Were we really in the dream?"

"We were," she said. "How real can a dream be . . . Well, we were, insofar as a dream can be real."

"What did you think of that dream? It's the first time for me, you know," I said.

"It was an ordinary dream," she said. "I told you, remember, that I go in and out of a lot of dreams like that. In other words, it was nothing special."

"That's what I think."

"I'm leaving," said the Dream Woman. "I'll come again."

"Are you going to a dream?"

"No. This is my time off. I want to take a walk around Mardin, see the markets," she said. "We'll see one another again. I'll come to you."

She left the room. I stood up and collected myself.

What interesting things had been happening to me ever since I set foot in Mardin. The black roses of Halfeti were vibrantly alive in the glass vase. My eyes sank into their velvet depths for a while. Suddenly I thought of the seer stone that King Darius had given me. I had forgotten it in my purse.

I searched through the bag and found the smooth, gleaming stone. It was so beautiful.

I slowly rotated it in my hand and looked at it.

IZMIR

"Your ankle is fine," said the doctor.

He was examining my ankle.

"You can leave the hospital now. You can relax at home. With a cane, you'll be able to walk. There's still some time before the cast comes off," he said.

I was unable to react happily to the news. I didn't know what to say. There was nowhere I could go with my leg in a cast in Izmir, no home where I could stay.

I sat on my bed in that ward without saying anything.

Mehdi the orderly said:

"What happened? All of a sudden your thoughts carried you away."

I was used to the ward. I was able to relax comfortably in bed. Outside was unknown, an enigma for me. The only connection I had to life in Izmir was Dr. Ayhan. He had done everything he could for me, what more could I ask?

I had to turn back and return, and if it were a dream, I had to wake up and come to myself.

But everything seemed real and concrete in this slice of time in which I was so strangely stuck. This Izmir, this hospital ward, this young doctor were just about as real as any number of parts of the life that I led in Ankara. I really couldn't figure out what to do at all. I was imprisoned in a slice of time belonging to the doctor's youth. I couldn't get out of this world. I couldn't say anything to anyone. I couldn't use my cell phone. It didn't work. I had tried it a few times.

Mehdi said:

"I'll get you ready to go really quickly. You don't have anything with you, anyway."

"Please let me leave before it gets dark," I said.

The doctor was scrutinizing me.

"Where are you going to go?" he asked.

"I don't have any place to go in this city."

"You had said that . . ."

"Maybe I'll stay in a pension until my foot gets straightened out."

"Something like that is impossible here," said the doctor. "A single woman can't stay alone in a pension!"

I was left speechless. I couldn't focus on anything.

"I'll talk to my mother," said the doctor. "I have an elderly mother. Maybe she can take you in as a guest for a few days. I think there's an extra room in the house. Let me talk to her. They should release you downstairs."

I looked with gratitude at the doctor's eyes. He took such interest in a patient. He didn't know who I was, where I came from, what I was doing in Izmir, anything at all.

Just like that, like the man who fell to earth, I had fallen into Izmir one early evening in 1949.

I thought to myself, "Dr. Ayhan's world. I'll be able to recognize him very well. But what good will that do? I don't live in 1949 Izmir! These aren't the years of my life."

It was a crazy thing, this 1949 Izmir, and young, handsome Dr. Ayhan there in front of me.

"Well, since I can't get out of this world, I might as well live it to the full," I said.

Suddenly I realized that I had been talking out loud. The dumpy attendant Mehdi was staring at me very closely.

"You can't leave this world," he said. "I realized that. I realized that you don't belong to this world, to these years. It was clear from the lighter you gave me. It's like you came from a space ship. From a flying saucer," he said. "The other day some villagers on the Narlıdere road saw a flying saucer. It was full of light. It dazzled their eyes and they fell down on the ground in fear. It's like you came out from inside that and came around here . . ."

"Help me get out of the bed," I said. "I have to walk around on my foot. How do we get released from here?"

"I'll bring the release paper to you," said Mehdi. "You just sit here and wait for me. It'll take a while. Forms and things . . . Stretch out on the bed. Don't let your ankle get swollen."

"Okay," I said.

I stretched out on the bed.

KING DARIUS

Someone tapped on my door. I woke up, and sat up amid the silk pillows. The sun had been shining for some time. The inside of my room at the Zinciriye Hotel was brightly lit. A bright, clear light was filtering through the thin embroidered curtains. Someone knocked gently at the door again.

"I'm coming!" I called out. I slipped something on and opened the door of my room.

Alop the slave was waiting outside the door.

"Excuse me," he said. "I woke you up."

"No problem. I had to wake up. I must have been tired . . ."

Alop the slave said:

"King Darius is overcome with excitement. That's why he sent me to you so early. They're going to get something at the palace this morning. You're supposed to know all about it."

I immediately remembered.

"Television!" I said. "King Darius wanted a television. Let's go and get it right away. You wait for me outside. I'll get dressed and come out."

Alop put a handful of gold coins in my hand.

"King Darius sent these," he said. "For expenses."

I looked at the coins he had stuck in my hand. They were pure gold coins. They had King Darius's portrait in relief on them.

"This is so much money!" I shouted. "What we're going to get doesn't cost this much."

"That's okay, just take them," said the slave. "After all, King Darius already sent them."

I took the gold coins and put them in a pocket of my purse.

"Wait for me."

A little later Alop the slave and I were in a shop that sold electronic equipment, in the center of the city.

The shop owner said:

"Ma'am. You want something that's the latest model. You know, one of those thin ones. They haven't come to Mardin yet. But we have very nice models. We'll give you a good price. If you want a console, I can give you a discount on it. If you want it mounted on the wall, we have a service that does that."

"Oh, this is nice," I said. "How large is it?"

"It's a 104-centimeter screen."

"Do you have one a little larger?"

"Here, this is 122 centimeters," said the man.

"There's not going to be any problem, is there? It's going to a very important place . . ."

"Please, ma'am," said the shopkeeper. "This is Mardin Arçelik here . . . There won't be any problem. We'll bring it right over and set it up, set up the antenna. You give me the address. We're including the console, aren't we?"

"Yes," I said. "The console with the glass."

I paused for a minute.

"It's going to the ruins of Dara," I said.

"Fine. I'm sending it right away. I'll send two men with it."

Alop the slave said:

"I'll go with them and show them the way."

I paid the money and bought the 122-centimeter plasma TV and the console.

"I'll put it in the van in a few minutes," said the shopkeeper. "The men will do the settings and connect it right up."

Alop the slave said:

"I'll keep an eye on them."

"Learn everything very well," I said to Alop the slave. "How the remotes work, where you press the buttons. Learn everything. The color settings . . ."

"We'll explain it to him, ma'am, don't worry," said the man.

Alop the slave got into the front of the van that pulled up. The two young men crowded in beside him. They hit the gas in the van and went off.

I was full of curiosity and excitement. I wondered how King Darius would feel when the television was set up and working.

I thought: "Let's not have him watch the regular television programs. I have to show King Darius some interesting things. He'll probably be amazed. His visual world has been limited to only the natural world."

From there I descended into the market that went down underground. I was still thinking about that ring with the purple stone. If I could find it, I would buy it.

WORLDS STILL THOUGHT TO EXIST

The four old men in the reception room prepared for the Night People in an apartment in Tunalı Hilmi Avenue were deeply engrossed in conversation. The gramophone was turned off, and Mermaid Ephtalia's voice was silenced. Everything was calm as the night continued outside. The few solitary people of the night were in the street, and the affairs of the night continued on in the darkness. A whistle like a watchman's whistle sounded every now and then. The night had spread out over the city, with all its freedom and also with all its restrictions and repression, going on naturally with perhaps absolutely no awareness that it was the most mysterious thing in the world.

The four old men in the night were each part of the night, and the approaching darkness, actually, but they didn't know this; maybe they sensed it, maybe the strength they expended to be tied to life and escape from their beds, to experience the night and freedom came from this.

Hıfzi Bey told them about old times. He told them about the days when some of the streets in Ankara were mud, the government office where he worked, the first time he saw his wife, and how excited he was when he got engaged.

"You're tied to your wife," said Dr. Ayhan. "You love her."

Hıfzi Bey thought for a minute.

"Habit," he said. "A habit you get used to over the years. I'm used to her quiet, interior sobbing when her feelings are hurt, the way she snores when she sleeps on her back in the bedroom, the way she carefully waters a row of plants by the window, her fears, her worries; I'm used to all of them. I couldn't change tracks when the time was right and make the effort to run off with my secretary, who was in love with me, and set up a love nest. I just stayed there, spineless, with no courage. But that girl was so pretty and she loved me so much."

"What happened to the girl?"

"She vanished into my memories, what do you expect?" said Hıfzi Bey.

"She left me. Abandoned me. I was destroyed. I went after her but I couldn't do a thing. The one at home was continuously crying.

"Between the two of them my life was poisoned. I have years I never lived; I want them back."

"You have years you never lived . . . That's a terrible phrase," said the doctor.

"Yes, I have years I never lived," said Hıfzi Bey. "I want them back! It's as though I didn't live for fifteen years. If they give those years back to me, I'd be sixty-nine years old. I'd be really young!"

"I have years I haven't lived too," said Şevki Bey.

Paying no attention to the fact that he was wearing a diaper, he threw one leg over the other as he sat in the armchair.

"I have twenty years I never lived. I didn't live for twenty years. Because I wasn't aware how life flows by. If they give me back those twenty years, I'll be sixty-two years old. I'll be young!" he shouted.

Mustafa Bey jumped in.

"I have thirty years I haven't lived, friends! At least thirty years. Years when I didn't know what life was, when I didn't comprehend that a person's days were numbered, when I just wasted my time . . . If they give me back those thirty years, I'd be around forty-eight now. Life would begin all over again for me. What an incredible thing!" he shouted. "I want my years back! Pay me back those years, give them to me!"

The doctor said:

"I have a lot of years I didn't live too.

"Maybe I've just started to live. Now I'm just thinking that

I started to live when I fell in love with that woman. If they give me back my years, I'll be a young man. A young doctor," he said. "I'd be at the age I was years ago, when I worked in the Konak Maternity Hospital in Izmir. The world would lie before me!"

The four old men were all excited.

"I wonder if they can give us those years back?" they were asking. "It's our right to get those years back. Where can we apply? Where can we learn whether or not we can get those years back?"

The chubby blonde entered the room.

"What's going on? What's happening?" she asked in curiosity. "What's all this excitement? What are you discussing?"

"We want the years we couldn't live back," said Şevki Bey. "The years we didn't notice, the years we lived without realizing their value . . ."

"Who's going to give them back to you?" asked the woman. "Is there any such thing? Unlived years . . . what does that mean?"

"Times that were just frittered away from our lives," said the doctor. "Years we lived without realizing them, years we were living and breathing . . ."

"Years taken out of our hands," said Şevki Bey. "Years spent for nothing, in other words."

The blonde women was thinking it over.

"Unlived years," she murmured. "There are years like that in my life too . . . the years I took care of my sick mother . . . years I was married to a man I didn't love . . ."

"How many years were there, roughly?" asked Mustafa Bey. A little adding machine emerged from his pocket.

The woman said:

"How should I know? There were maybe twenty years altogether like that. That you could say were unlived. Years my husband beat me . . . bonds that took years away from my life . . . twenty, twenty-five years."

Mustafa Bey said:
"Wait, let me calculate it. How old are you now?"
"Fifty," said the woman.
"You could be thirty years old," said Mustafa Bey.
"Thirty years old!" cried the woman.
"If you take away the years you couldn't live, the years they took from you, you would be thirty years old."
"Youth!" shouted the blonde woman. "When I was on top of everything; the years when life hadn't pressed me down!"
"Well that's it," said Mustafa Bey.
"Well, how can we get those spent years back? How do we do it? Where do we get them?" asked the woman.
"That's what we're figuring out," said Hıfzi Bey from where he sat. "Where to apply."
The doctor said:
"Oh, if I could go back to those long ago years of mine. I'd found love too. I was crazy with desire for her. Always on my mind. Who knows what I would do if I could go back to those years, to Izmir, to my years at the Konak Maternity Hospital . . . ?"

MARDIN

I had gone back to my hotel room. I was thinking of going back to the Dara ruins after I rested a little and tidied up. There was a minibus that went to the ruins from the bus stop; I had seen it when I was coming in.
I bought the purple ring in the shopping passage. It was on my finger.
The seer stone was in my hand. I had been turning it over and over since yesterday. Nothing at all happened. It was just a gleaming, transparent stone. It was probably broken. I have to tell King Darius about it. It was obvious the stone wasn't working. I tossed it into my purse.
There was a knock on the door of my room.

"Come in," I said.

The door crept open. The Dream Woman slowly slipped in. She looked very nice. Her wavy blonde hair was a little in disarray, and she had a black velvet gown on. She was barefoot. I saw her shapely white feet and her toenails painted with red polish.

"Come in, come in," I said. "Where have you been?"

"Please, don't even ask," she said. She sat down on the edge of the bed.

"I'm coming from the dream of the Spanish director Luis Buñuel. I'm completely dazed. What a world that is! For one thing, it was very hard to get into; you know that curtain at the end of the passageway, well, when you go into Buñuel's, it's made out of snakeskin. It must be special order. It's a strange thing, slimy, repulsive, and grisly. Wet. Like pushing aside some huge snake to go inside. But very erotic. I felt strange. It's a dark world, and his dream is too. I went through ancient Catalan cemeteries, and there was a grave whose cover had slid loose and the jet-black hair of a woman was flowing out from the grave. I shrank back in horror. There were statues of male and female saints, a courtyard. I just couldn't get to Buñuel's dream. Women, men, film workers, a film set . . . At one point I got past that too. Long, long lanes, bordered with dark cypresses.

"Just as I was thinking, 'The best thing to do would be to just go back, to get out of this dream,' I went right into a church. There was a Mass going on. I sat down in one of the back pews and listened to an aria sung by a young black nun in a contralto voice. I suddenly felt emotional. I was about to cry. When the aria finished, I slowly went outside. This strange world had just swallowed me up inside it. I was going around in it, but there was no sign of Buñuel.

"There was a blonde woman sitting in a huge leather chair. The kind who's cold as ice. Just an armchair there in the middle of the air. The woman was sitting. She looked down at me.

A half-full glass of whiskey in her hand. She gave me a look.

"'Who are you?' she said in a caustic voice.

"'The Black Rose of Halfeti!' I blurted out. It just came out of my mouth. The woman was surprised by the name. I could tell by her eyes.

"'Where are you coming from?' she asked me.

"'The last place was Mardin,' I said.

"She was completely astonished.

"'What are you looking for in Mardin?' she asked in amazement.

"'I walk around there,' I said. What was I supposed to say?

"The woman responded, 'What are you walking around here for? Who are you looking for?'

"'I'm looking for Luis Buñuel,' I said.

"She suddenly got up from her armchair.

"'What do you want with him?' she yelled.

"'I went into his dream,' I stuttered.

"'You can't go into his dream,' the woman shouted. 'Just any woman can't go into his dream.'

"'Why not?' I said. 'Dreams are open to everyone. As far as I know.'

"'No, go back outside,' said the woman. 'You cannot go into Buñuel's dream!'

"'Who are you?' I asked.

"'I'm Silvia Pinal,' she said.

"I had never heard this name before.

"'Are you his wife?'

"'I'm his lover,' she said.

"The woman was jealous. She was going to cause a scene. I realized that. I was about to go back when I heard a voice behind me.

"'Who were you looking for?' it was asking. I turned and looked, Buñuel. A dark man. He was leaning against the trunk of a tall beech tree and looking at me.

"'Come closer, please,' he said.

"I was frightened. He was very strange.

"'Silvia Pinal is getting angry,' I said.

"Buñuel smiled.

"'Forget about Silvia Pinal,' he said.

"I slowly walked over to him. I had come under the beech tree. He took me by the hands and pulled me toward him. He buried his head in my shoulder and in my hair. He smelled me as you would smell a flower. As though he was drawing my scent into his lungs. Then he slowly released my body. I felt like I had gone into a river and come out.

"'Okay, leave,' he said. 'Be careful when you go by the cemetery.'

"I was very affected by him. He smelled of tobacco and gunpowder. It was hard for me to leave there. His odor remained in my nostrils. I ran back on the roads that I had come on. I ran with all my strength as I passed by the Catalan graveyard. The graves had changed. It was as though I were on a different path, and I suddenly felt death. There, in that century-old graveyard. I ran as fast as I could.

"I got to the snakeskin hanging across the passageway. It was wet. It was a masculine thing, difficult to explain. I slowly pushed it aside and came out. I was shaking like crazy.

"I've never experienced anything like this in a man's dream in my entire life. I really reacted to it."

The Dream Woman was in a state of excitement.

"It's not easy to go into Buñuel's dreams," I said.

"You have no idea how upset I was," she said. "That half-dark world. Those ancient, shadowy memories. I think they were in Spain, that blonde woman. The cemetery . . . that revulsion I felt there. The way I ran through those unending labyrinths, and Buñuel . . . It was completely other," she murmured.

"A male scent. Tenderness. Strength and searching. That short embrace he gave me."

She stopped for a minute.

"I'm going to go into his dream again," she said.

"I want to run straight to him through those worlds again."

She paused.

"That damp thing at the end of the passageway," she said. "You know, that curtain . . . Maybe that was part of Buñuel. Warm and wet . . ."

She stretched out on the bed and closed her eyes.

"You go into so many men's dreams," I said.

"But this man had an effect on me," she murmured.

THE BLACK ROSE OF HALFETI

She had stretched out on the bed. Her head was buried in my pillow, and the black gown radiated out over the pure white sheets. Her eyes were half closed. I gazed at her for a while. She looked so beautiful, so alluring.

"If I go into Buñuel's dream right now, would it be a mistake?" she asked me spontaneously.

"You were just there," I said.

"I know, but I miss him," she said. "In a strange way I want to see him again."

"Then rush right into his dream," I said.

She sat up from where she had been reclining.

"Should I really do that?"

"Hurry up, go in."

She got up from the bed. She fixed her hair in front of the mirror.

"I'm going," she said.

"How will you get in?"

"I'll go in through the jetway corridor."

"What if he's awake?"

"He's asleep, I know," she said. "I have to get in before he wakes up. Let me catch him!"

She ran out the door.

The Dream Woman had fallen for Buñuel.

I lay down on the couch, and rested my head on the silk cushions.

The ceiling of the room was so high and airy.

Looking around, I was imagining things, half-asleep and half-awake. A thousand and one things were going through my mind. I had asked for a rose sherbet a little while ago and the waiter brought it. I took a sip of the sherbet. The seer stone was in my hand. It was still shiny and transparent, with nothing inside.

I must tell King Darius about this. The stone must be defective. I still hadn't seen a thing inside it.

I was slowly stroking it, and my eyelids became heavy.

Suddenly a tiny movement in the stone caught my eye. It was just a little flicker. It might have been the shadow of my face.

Now I looked more carefully into the seer stone. I saw the Dream Woman. The picture became quite clear, and as I massaged the stone with my fingers, the image drew nearer and receded. I noticed in surprise that the transparent stone, the crystal ball in my hand, was like the screen on a cell phone.

I shouldn't have been surprised at all by the stone. It was like the twin of the cell phone in my purse. I was carrying around what was virtually the same thing in my purse, so there was no reason for me to be amazed by this magical stone.

I carefully began to follow the image in the stone. The Black Rose of Halfeti was running in the darkness, down a narrow road bordered on either side by tall cypresses. It must be a side road in a Catholic cemetery. It was so creepy and depressing. It reminded me of a painting that had been hanging on the wall of an old house for years.

The woman was out of breath; she had gathered up her skirts and was running quickly down the narrow cobblestoned path.

Suddenly the cypresses opened up. Now, across the way, I saw Silvia Pinal sitting in a large Morocco leather chair.

Silvia Pinal was wearing a black silk slip, and her blonde hair fell down over her shoulders.

"What are you looking for here?" she shouted at the Black Rose of Halfeti.

"What are you hanging around here for, you piece of trash? Didn't I tell never to come here again?"

She dashed the whiskey in the crystal glass in her hand in the woman's face.

At that instant, rain started to pour down inside the seer stone. I saw how the lightning lit up all the veins of the stone.

It was an extraordinary sight. Suddenly Buñuel appeared. He was leaning against the thick trunk of a beech tree, surveying the scene.

When he saw the Dream Woman, he opened his arms. The woman flung herself into his arms like a ball that has been thrown quickly, and she wrapped her arms around his neck. As another flash of lighting came from the electricity between them. At that moment a bolt of lightning struck the beech tree with a great roar. The tree turned into ashes.

Buñuel took the woman's face between his hands and stared into her eyes. They were unaware of anything else. They hadn't noticed the lightning bolt. The rain had fallen on both of them, and they were soaking wet.

What an incredible scene this was. Something unbelievable. Buñuel and the Dream Woman were embracing inside the seer stone, just standing there. Buñuel leaned down and kissed her on her lips.

I stared in great excitement at Buñuel and the Dream Woman in their close embrace inside the seer stone. The half of the beech tree that still stood was charred as black as coal. The other half was a mass of ashes that the falling rain was washing away down the narrow path.

"She's in love with Buñuel," I murmured to myself. "This must be what they call lightning love."

The image in the seer stone started to cloud over slightly. A little later it became very unclear and vanished. The stone reverted to its former state.

I would not forget the unbelievable image I had seen for the rest of my life, I knew that. The beech tree next to the cemetery, the rain pouring down, and a man and a woman in an embrace . . .

"What's going on?" I thought. "What happens in dreams . . . But maybe what I saw was real."

What I had seen in the seer stone didn't seem like a dream. It must have been real.

I slowly closed my eyes.

KING DARIUS AND THE GLOBAL ADAPTOR

I must have overslept. When I awoke, it was well after noon. I quickly got up and dressed. I checked the seer stone; it was transparent, still and gleaming, with no images inside. I placed it carefully in my purse. My cell phone was turned off. I turned it on and glanced at the incoming messages. There was an account summary from the bank and an invitation from the perfume store on Tunalı Hilmi for skin care. Also an advertisement for a new perfume that had just come on the market.

The new perfume was called "Enchanting Love." I turned off the phone again and dropped it into my purse.

I went upstairs to the terrace to get something to eat.

That incomparable view of Mesopotamia spread out before me. As I sipped my coffee, I looked at the peaceful, quiet view, at the nearby minaret of the Şehidiye Mosque, and at the line of the horizon that disappeared in the distant sands of the desert.

Alop the slave silently came up the steps and stood there by my side.

"Alop!" I cried, startled. "I didn't notice you. When did you come?"

"I came just now," said Alop. "You were having breakfast, and I didn't want to disturb you."

"I've finished my breakfast."

"I'll take you to the palace. King Darius is waiting. They set up the television."

"How is it, is it working?" I asked out of curiosity.

"It's working," said Alop the slave. "The pictures came up. King Darius has the remote in his hand and wants to ask you some questions."

"Let's go to the palace right now," I said.

Shortly afterward we arrived at King Darius's palace. Alop the slave took me by the arms and pulled me up into the dark room on top of the earthwork walls.

There was a team working in the archeological site in the distance. That section of the archeological area had been closed to visitors. An ancient tomb had been discovered. The archeologists were all excited. They were looking at the top of the stone sarcophagus visible in the deep pit they had dug. I wanted so much to be there and learn to whom this grave that they had discovered belonged. I had heard that they were unearthing statues and graves, one more interesting than the next, in the ongoing excavations in the Dara ruins.

They hadn't yet informed anyone about these discoveries that illuminated this period of history. They were still quite new, and there was no one around except a not very large number of individuals interested in one or two old grave chambers and the skeletons inside them. I was able to get information from the little village girls who played all day long among the ruins.

When I first came to the ruins three days ago, they told me that a glass crown belonging to the queen and a valuable ring had been found in a large burial chamber that had been opened.

"The crown was made of glass. When they washed it, it was gleaming in the sunlight," the little girls said in excitement.

They spent most of their days in the Dara ruins. They knew the places where the archeologists had excavated, the burial chambers and the statues they found. The lives of the little girls were mingling with the lives of people who had lived in these ruins thousands of years ago, as though they were an inseparable part of their everyday lives.

I was walking behind Alop the slave down the hall that led to the splendid stone hall where King Darius's throne stood. The air was very hot. It felt even hotter in the ruins.

The sounds of men's and women's voices came to my ear.

I looked at Alop the slave.

"Does King Darius have guests?"

"No, madame. Those voices are coming from the television," said the slave.

I moved ahead, filled with curiosity, and reached King Darius's broad terrace.

Alop the slave said:

"The king is over on the side, in his chamber. The men who came from Mardin Arçelik set up the television there. They plugged in something they called a 'global adaptor' to the wall there. The put up an antenna on the left-hand side of the ruins. They concealed it a little next to the stones. They pulled in something called electricity from the Dara Café, by the gate of the ruins. I asked the men who came, and I learned all these things so I could explain them to you."

"Thank you very much, Alop," I said. "You've learned marvelous things. That 'global adaptor' must be something new. It's the first time I've heard of it."

"They attached it to the wall," said Alop the slave. "It can be used anywhere in the world and regulates the electricity. I think it's being used in our palace because it suits our world, the world in which we live."

"That must be it," I said.

It must be an adaptor that connects this world and the other world, I thought to myself.

So then television could work in this very old palace that belonged to centuries past. And they pulled in the electricity from the little café next to the ruins. Its name was the Dara

Café, and it had two tables and chairs. The first day I came I was thirsty and had a fruit soda there. I bought cookies and chewing gum for the little girls who were showing me around the ruins.

We were advancing along the hall.

There were sounds coming from King Darius's rooms. It was obvious the king was playing with the remote, as though he were channel surfing. The clouds of sound and conversation were swirling around and moving in the air, providing an incredibly strange atmosphere in the darkness of the stone cavity. For a moment it seemed to me that the centuries old walls around me had started to speak and were talking to each other.

I slowly entered the room where King Darius was. They had put the television in the corner. It looked very nice on top of the little table.

King Darius heard me come in. He turned to me.

"Welcome!" he said.

"I'm very excited. This is an extraordinary thing! Astonishing, unbelievable. The young man who set it up taught me how to change the channels, but I haven't quite mastered it yet. When you touch it the picture changes very quickly."

"Give me the remote and I'll show you," I said.

The plasma screen was shining like the sun in the corner of the ancient stone walls. I took the remote in my hands and started to press the buttons randomly.

The television came to life.

THE SALON FOR THE NIGHT PEOPLE

The old doctor, Hıfzi Bey, Mustafa the accountant, and Şevki Bey were sitting in the salon prepared for the Night People and chattering energetically.

"I feel so peaceful in this salon," said Hıfzi Bey. "I'm relaxed here. It's as though I lived my whole life in a living room like this. The room where my mother received her friends on her at-home day looked like this; when I first married we had a room like this in our house too, even the colors were the same."

"I said the same thing," said the old doctor. "My house was the same as this too. The china cabinet in the corner with the mirror, the glasses inside it . . . that carpet on the floor. Just like my house."

"That picture of the pasha on the wall," said Şevki Bey. "It's just like my dear departed father. The same eyebrows, the same piercing eyes, the same big moustache. I ask myself, 'Is that him?' I wonder, is my late father here with us?"

"Does he look like your father?" asked Mustafa Bey.

"Exactly the same. Like his twin. He's caught my eye. It seems like he follows every move I make."

"Was your father a pasha?" asked the old doctor.

"He was a colonel."

"This one is a colonel too," said the doctor. "So it must be your father."

"I can't be exactly sure," said Şevki Bey. "I've forgotten my father after all these years. I forgot what he looked like in his old colonel's uniform."

Mustafa Bey joined in.

"That isn't a colonel. It's a general, a pasha," he said. He continued to speak. "What's going to become of the years we didn't live? Let's not forget about that."

"Would we?" said the old doctor. "We'll get those years back. But first we have to find out who that picture on the wall is."

"Right," said Mustafa Bey. "We have to identify him."

Hıfzi Bey said:

"He's here with us every night in this room. I wonder if it's the former owner of this place."

"I have no idea," said Şevki Bey. "My father never had a house like this."

"Allah, Allah, who could it be?" asked Hıfzi Bey.

"Like I said, he looks a lot like my father, but I can't be sure," said Şevki Bey.

The four old men stared for a long time at the picture on the wall.

"If we only knew who it was . . . ," Hıfzi Bey said.

"I wonder how we can find out who this pasha belongs to?" Şevki Bey asked.

"I'm dying of curiosity," said Hıfzi Bey. "I wonder from whom we could learn who this pasha is?"

The blonde woman came in.

"Gentlemen, I brought you tea," she said. "I just brewed it."

She put the cups of tea that she'd carried in on a decorated tray down on a low table.

"Excuse me, I'd like to ask you something," said Hıfzi Bey.

"Of course."

"I wonder who that pasha on the wall is, do you know him?"

The woman stared for a time at the picture of the pasha on the wall.

"I don't know him at all. That picture was hanging on the wall when I came here. I have no idea as to who it could be."

"It's a pasha," said the old doctor. "We thought, who knows, maybe you know who he was."

"Unfortunately, I have no information about who the pasha is," said the woman.

"Well, let's talk about the years we never lived," said Hıfzi Bey. "Where can we get them back from? Where do we have to apply, I wonder?"

"I'll look into all of that," said the woman. "The more I think about it, the more the number of years I never lived goes up. It's unbelievable. I'll get back almost to my twenties. It's really amazing."

Şevki Bey said:

"A whole bunch of details about my life came to mind. If I collect them all together, it would come to a few years more. Well, a few years in a person's life are very important. A loose tooth, losing hair, a bald spot on the top. These are things that happen in a few years. I could even go back farther than that. I'm making up a list." He went on, "Isn't that the way it is? An ear that doesn't hear well, an aching knee . . . A person could escape from all of them if we could get those years back . . ."

"We'll get those years we didn't live back," said Mustafa Bey. "Just like setting a clock back."

The tea was finished.

A strange sound came from the wall.

They all looked in that direction.

KING DARIUS AND THE GLOBAL ADAPTOR

I was trying to line up the channels one after another.

King Darius asked, "Which one should we pick? What should we look at? There's a part with blonde women. Women who all have shiny blonde hair. They're in one place. Somewhere around there. In one place . . ."

"What's that, I wonder? I hadn't noticed. Which program?"

"If you press it again, they'll come."

I pushed down on the remote control again.

"Oh, see, there they are!" said King Darius.

What was being shown on the screen was a concert with the Istanbul Municipal Conservatory Chorus and an Oriental *saz* ensemble.

All of the women were dressed in black. They were of a certain age, mostly with blonde or platinum hair. Looking at the notes in front of them, they were singing a slow piece that was, I think, in the Hüzzam mode.

They all looked meticulously dressed, with pearl necklaces around their necks, rings on their fingers, rouge, and nail polish.

King Darius was looking at them in complete admiration.

I was looking with a fresh eye at this music and the images on the screen that had never previously interested me.

"The women are very beautiful," said King Darius. "They're singing a song."

"Yes . . . It's a song in the Hüzzam mode. It's the Istanbul Municipal Conservatory Chorus and a *saz* ensemble," I said.

Alop the slave was standing to the side. He couldn't pull his eyes off the screen.

"Your Majesty, Darius," I said. "May I take your eyes away from the screen for a moment?"

"What are you going to do?" he asked. "They sing so beautifully."

"They'll be back again. I was going to look at something. With your permission."

"I give you permission," said King Darius.

Playing quickly with the buttons on the remote, I went back to the advertisement that had caught my eye a moment ago.

"Uğur Dündar and *Arena* tonight. 'Organ Mafia,' kidneys for sale, Indian kidney market . . . Dr. Necip Yağmur talks to Uğur Dündar. Tonight on *Arena*."

King Darius listened closely to what was being said on the screen.

"What's all this?" he asked.

"It's a program I think you'll find interesting," I said.

"Who was that man? They showed him, and now is he talking and explaining things?" he asked.

"He's a very famous television personality, newspaperman, and writer: Uğur Dündar," I said.

The king was listening carefully to what I said.

"A television personality," he repeated. "He's inside the television; he doesn't come out, right?"

"No, dear, he comes out," I said. "He's someone just like you and me. He goes around outside. The television is an image. I don't know how to explain it . . ."

"I understand," said King Darius. "It's like the seer stone . . ."

"Perhaps," I said.

I suddenly recalled Buñuel's incomparable dream that I had seen in the seer stone. The seer stone was more natural, it was even more difficult to understand. Maybe the images seen in the seer stone were composed of messages transferred from one brain to another by currents and signals.

"These programs on the television are filmed in a studio," I said.

"So that's it," said King Darius. "What's a studio?"

"It's a place where the people and filming instruments connect with television and where special lights are located."

"Little by little I will learn all of these things," said King Darius. "Right now, let's go back to those women. The ones who were just there."

I played with the remote.

The women's chorus came back on the screen again.

They had gone on to a different song now. King Darius and Alop the slave began to watch them with admiration.

THE PASHA

Everyone was quiet in the half-dark salon of the Night People. That room that confined scenes from people's pasts was now in silence. The four old men sitting in the armchairs heard the cough coming from the portrait of the pasha on the wall.

The framed picture of the pasha cleared its throat once again.

It began to speak in a deep bass voice.

"Something's caught in my throat. May I ask for a glass of water?"

"I'll bring it right away," said the blonde woman.

She jumped up and rushed to the kitchen. She came back a little later with a glass of water in her hand.

"Here you are, Pasha."

"Thank you, my girl," said the pasha. "Would you help me drink it?"

"Of course, Pasha."

The woman slowly raised the glass to the pasha's lips. After the pasha took a few sips of water, he slowly pulled back a little.

"Thank you, my girl," he said.

"My pleasure, Pasha."

The four old men were staring in complete amazement at the portrait of the pasha from where they sat.

The woman gently asked:

"Are you going to speak today, Pasha?"

"There's a lot to say," said the pasha.

"There are so many things to tell . . . Things that have accumulated inside, memories that occupy my mind. Many things that I felt and heard in this room . . . But I'm not going to speak anymore today; I think I'll just listen."

"Fine, Pasha."

The pasha became silent.

His eyes were fixed on some point off in eternity. He had receded back into the gilt frame of the painting, lost in his own world.

A little later Hıfzi Bey said:

"Did he really talk?"

Mustafa Bey answered:

"He drank water and talked."

Dr. Ayhan was confused.

Şevki Bey rearranged the diaper that was making his pajamas bulge.

"The painting came to life and talked," he said. "This is the strangest thing that's ever happened to me in my whole life."

"It's unbelievable," said Hıfzi Bey.

Doctor Ayhan said:

"This pasha must be a part of this night that we're lost in, where we just hold on to one of the edges. Something like that . . . This night, this salon, they're all a part of it."

The blonde woman nodded her head. "Yes," she said. "You're

quite right. The pasha is part of the night, the darkness, and this room."

"Does he talk once in a while?"

"Sometimes he talks," said the woman.

"How mysterious," muttered the old doctor. "If only he had talked a little more."

"Maybe he'll talk tomorrow night," said the woman.

"Let's ask the pasha about the unlived years too," said Şevki Bey. "Maybe he can give us an opinion. I wonder where we can get those unlived years back from?"

Hıfzi Bey said:

"It's like a dream. To go back . . . to collect the old years, to make a bouquet of them and get to use them again. Will we be able to get those years back?"

"We will," said the old doctor. "We'll get them back somehow."

The room became quiet.

Outside, in Tunalı, there was no one.

A cat screeched. It was a howl that reminded people of their childhood.

The old men had become silent. Maybe they were asleep.

The woman went into the back, poured the tea that had been boiling all night in the teapot down the sink, and put fresh tea on to brew.

It was clear she was getting ready for the morning.

Faint daylight was about to filter through the sheer curtains.

THE BLACK ROSE OF HALFETI

I was in my room in the Zinciriye Hotel in Mardin. I had no idea what time it was. Last night I'd watched Uğur Dündar's *Arena* program until the late hours with King Darius in the palace. It was fabulous. It was the first time that I had watched a program like *Arena* through the eyes of an eminent emperor like King Darius, who had no knowledge of the new world, who didn't even know what an organ was.

The subject of *Arena* last night was the "Organ Mafia." Uğur Dündar was explaining the organ traffickers whose trail he had been able to locate and describing how organ trafficking worked. For the last segment, he put on the air live a Dr. Necdet Nacar, known as "Dr. Frankenstein," who performs illegal kidney transplants for millions of dollars in an unnamed hospital abroad. Visible live in a box in a corner of the screen with his green surgical uniform and mask was Dr. Necdet Nacar, who gave evasive answers to Uğur Dündar's questions, speaking aggressively due to the anxiety he felt because the master journalist had located him and put him on screen, and he skipped off before the broadcast was finished.

King Darius followed Uğur Dündar's program with unbelievable curiosity and excitement. The kidneys taken from healthy people abroad, the Indian connection, poor Indians lying down on operating beds to sell their kidneys, the "Organ Mafia" that steals children's kidneys, the lengthy line of ill people who see Dr. Necdet Nacar as a beacon of hope, the agreements for transplants made in a high-end bar in Dubai in the middle of the night, the money given to the doctor in a bag, the transportation of the removed kidneys to the hospital, the comments made by a patient about to die from an infection into a microphone held out by Uğur Dündar . . .

The program was fascinating, the investigation, the revelations, the brief comments by Dr. Necdet Nacar from behind the operating table, the money being counted, the kidneys taken from corpses, the untrustworthy fat man in charge of the whole thing. What a slender young girl lying in a room in a mansion on Büyükada said into Uğur Dündar's microphone . . .

"These are such overwhelming things!" cried King Darius. "Illegal things!"

The king was amazed by Uğur Dündar.

"I want to meet him," he said. "I have to get to know him. He's an incredible man. Powerful."

"Yes, he is."

"Kidney? What's a kidney?" said King Darius. "Tell me about kidneys. What does a kidney do? Do I have one? Do you have one too? Why are they so valuable? Look, these people are consuming one another over kidneys."

"I'll tell you all about it," I said. "The kidney is an organ essential for life. If it doesn't work, a person would die!"

"Oh!" said King Darius. "I had no idea about such a thing. A kidney."

"Wait till tomorrow, Your Majesty," I said. "I'll tell you everything little by little. There's a lung too . . . a heart . . ."

"What are they?"

"They're organs too."

King Darius stopped for a minute.

"I have to learn the organs," he said. "Kidney, lung, heart . . ."

"Eye," I said.

I was getting sleepy.

Arena ended at a late hour.

I took leave of King Darius and went back to my hotel. I got into bed and immediately fell into a deep sleep. The weather must have turned warm. I woke toward morning and turned over a little in my bed.

I felt there was someone in my room.

Buñuel might have come. I sat up in bed.

I picked out the Black Rose of Halfeti in the semi-dark room. She was sitting silently at the foot of my bed. She was wearing her magnificent black velvet gown and had strands of pearls around her neck.

When she saw that I was awake, she leaned over toward me.

"I woke you up," she said.

"No matter, did something happen?" I asked.

"No, no. Nothing important," she said. "We've been called to dreams. Morning dreams. Both of us. I came to get you."

"We've been called to dreams?"

"Yes. We're going into morning dreams."

I had gotten out of bed and was trying to put myself together.

"Whose dreams are we supposed to go into?" I asked. At the same time, I had turned on the light and was combing my hair in front of the mirror.

"You're going into the old doctor's dream," said the Black Rose of Halfeti. "He spent the night in Ankara in a salon for the Night People in Tunalı Hilmi, and he's sleeping now."

"Oh," I said. "And you?"

"I'm supposed to go into a pasha's dream. Come on, get ready. Let's go together," she said.

"What pasha?"

I was curious.

"Some former pasha," she said. "He's connected somehow with that salon where the Night People get together. I don't have all the details. I'll learn them when I get into the dream."

"And I'm going into the old doctor's dream?" I asked.

"Yes, he particularly wants you in his morning dream, apparently. You know morning dreams are very influential and important."

She paused for a minute.

"Dear," she said. "Let the man do whatever he wants in the dream. Don't run away from him. After all, it's just a dream . . . Nothing in it means anything, you know. If he wants to kiss you and such, just let him do it. In fact, if he wants to go even farther, just let him. Let him live his dream."

I started to laugh.

A little later I was dressed. The Black Rose of Halfeti and I left the room together.

THE MORNING DREAM

We walked through the passageway that wobbled under my feet and got to the doorway that looked like the entrance to a cockpit. The young female attendant was there.

"You will go in first," she said to me. "When that light turns green go in slowly. You know, not too much excitement, nothing extreme, no sudden movements."

"Fine," I said.

The Black Rose of Halfeti was standing next to me.

She was fixing her hair with her hand, fiddling with her pearl necklace.

"The pasha?" she asked the young female attendant. "Who is this pasha?"

"A pasha," said the official. "He's in a painting at the moment. Captive, in other words . . . But there's nothing to worry about. You'll go right into his morning dream."

"Do they listen to the conversation?" asked the Black Rose of Halfeti.

"Be careful, and take care," said the young woman. "That's all I can tell you."

The Black Rose of Halfeti turned to me. "Did you see that?" she said. "I swear, a person could get in trouble. I don't know what to do. Maybe they listen to us in dreams."

She was tense.

"What if I don't go into the dream?"

"I don't know," I said.

"Well, after all, the pasha is captive in a painting," said the attendant on duty.

"The place where you're going to meet with him is in a dream. These are abstract things . . . ," continued the attendant.

"Fine. Then I'll go in . . ."

The green light lit up.

"You go in first," the young woman said to me.

I slowly opened the curtain covering the cockpit and looked

inside. The old doctor was sitting in an armchair. His face seemed to light up when he saw me.

THE SALON OF THE NIGHT PEOPLE

I saw that strange, old-fashioned salon where the Night People gathered for the first time when I went into the old doctor's dream just before dawn. Aside from the doctor, there were three other old men and a plump blonde woman in this Night Salon. The woman seemed to be taking care of the old men, continually bringing them something to eat or drink.

I was in the dream. The old doctor stood up from his armchair.

"Welcome," he said. "You didn't disappoint me; you're here. Let me introduce you to my friends. Mustafa Bey, Şevki Bey, and Hıfzı Bey . . . We've been getting together here at nighttime for a while."

The woman said, "My name is Nilüfer. Please, sit down there."

A morning coffee was immediately put in front of me.

The old doctor was very happy. I could see the pleasure in his eyes.

This room, this old-fashioned salon brought back so many memories to me. The salon in my mother's house on Yüksel Avenue in Ankara, the guest room in my grandmother's house in Kızıltoprak in Istanbul . . . the color of the curtains, the armchairs, the low tables scattered here and there, the mirrored buffet in the corner . . . Everything was somewhat familiar, things I was accustomed to. The frosted glass ashtrays that looked like my mother's ashtrays, whole sets of old-fashioned thin crystal glasses, goblets, and a set of water glasses in the buffet with glass doors, coffee cups with princesses with pink skirts in relief and delicate gold leaf around the edges. My eyes picked out the bibelots of my childhood in the dark corners of the salon . . .

The old men were excitedly telling me something.

The old man whose name I learned was Hıfzi said:

"We were talking before you came. There are years in our lives that we never lived. Years that go by without a person being aware of them, years that amounted to nothing. We counted them up. Everybody has some. Fifteen years, twenty years . . . If we could just get them back, we could start our lives with those years and move forward. We realized this here, in these hours of the night. We're after those unlived years of ours."

The old doctor turned to me. "If I could get my hands on those unlived years, I'd be very young," he said.

He smiled at me very meaningfully.

UNLIVED YEARS

The unlived years that these old men were thinking about as they sat in this strange Night Salon intrigued me.

The old man in pajamas named Şevki said:

"Look, it caught your interest too. I could tell from your expression."

Truly, these "unlived years" had caught my interest.

"Years that weren't noticed," said Şevki Bey.

"So then, the years of youth," I said.

"Yes, it could be the young years," he said.

I became lost in thought. I must have unlived years too. I wondered which ones they were.

"A person doesn't notice the young years when they're young," said the blonde woman. "Youth passes like a dream and disappears. Only after it's gone does a person realize what youth is."

She took a little breath.

"Prison years, years dragged out in a bad marriage, years of illness," said the old doctor. "Years spent in treatment."

"Yes," I said. "These are all years that are unlived. True. Fine, well who gives these years back?"

"That's what we're trying to find out," said Hıfzi Bey. "If we could only find that person . . ."

"Maybe some organization gives them back," said Şevki Bey. "It might be an organizational kind of thing. Then we would go and claim our rights from this organization."

The old doctor didn't take his eyes off of me.

I realized that my presence there that night in the Night Salon gave him great happiness.

He slowly bent over to my ear. "I ran away from home last night," he whispered. "I've broken all my ties with my past. I'm free now. Even if it's late, I'm free. I wanted you to know that.

"They're looking for me now. But they won't find me. I'm not going back home. I'm happy here. You'll come to me once in a while, won't you?" he asked. "You'll come, right? Here, to this salon?"

"I will," I said.

His face seemed to relax.

A signal light above us started to flash.

I raised my head and looked at it.

An arrow that said "Exit" was blinking.

I realized that it was time for me to leave the morning dream.

Suddenly I found myself in the wobbly corridor without having said goodbye to anyone.

The Black Rose of Halfeti was at my side.

"What happened all of a sudden?" I asked. "I just found myself here helter-skelter."

"The dream ended," said the young woman. "The doctor must have woken up. You left the dream."

"What did you do with the pasha?"

"The pasha is an incredible person," said the Black Rose of Halfeti. "I talked to him about Luis Buñuel. I told him how I was in love with Buñuel. I told him all about those unusual emotions I experienced, the moment when I saw Buñuel leaning against the beech tree waiting for me, the lightning striking the tree, the way I ran in fear through the Catalan graves, everything."

"Fine, well what did the pasha say?"

"He listened to me with a sweet smile on his face.

"'How lovely. You're telling me about love and passion,' he said. 'Just like in a film . . . Come to me again, tell me these unusual dreams and about these worlds that I don't know, okay?'

"'Of course I'll come,' I said.

"That means he wasn't bored. He was listening to me in total admiration."

"Is the pasha really captive?" I asked the Black Rose of Halfeti.

"Yes, captive," the girl said. "A captive pasha. Inside the four walls of a gilt frame."

"Well then, what was his crime?"

"He didn't tell me."

KING DARIUS

"Where's my kidney?" asked King Darius. He was feeling his midriff and back with his hand.

"There, Your Majesty," I said. "You have two kidneys. Here and there."

"Hmm," muttered King Darius. "On my two sides . . . I understand. Well, where's my liver?"

"Your liver is there, Your Majesty."

He felt the place where the liver was.

"So my liver is here?"

"Yes."

"These are important organs . . ."

"Very important organs," I said. "That's why they pay a lot of money for them."

"Yes. But it's a horrible thing to sell them. Stealing them is horrible too," said Darius. "Where is the heart?"

"Just here."

"The brain?"

"Inside your head."

Darius said:

"I'm going to give this a good thinking over. I've been living with these organs for years, and before I watched that program I had no idea they even existed. Well, these organs are inside, what do they look like? How do they find them and remove or connect them in their places?"

"King Darius, this is a completely different subject. We'll speak about that in good time. I'll try to explain it to you as best I can."

"Fine," said King Darius. "Sometimes I have a pain here."

I looked at the place where he pointed.

"Your stomach," I said.

"Yes, it aches once in a while," he said. "After meals."

"I'll give you a tablet to chew; it might help."

King Darius was amazed.

"All the things I'm learning!" he said. The stomach . . . stomach aches and a tablet that cures it. There are all these things that I didn't know about in the world. It's as though I moved into a second world after I got that television."

I was thinking that, truly, an incredible second world had revealed itself to King Darius.

"I want to know and learn everything," he said. "I don't want to miss all this innovation, all these exciting things. I'm a powerful king. I own all of these lands. And I want to possess all of this knowledge as well. How can we do this?"

I was trying to think.

"Maybe you could go to a school," I said.

He immediately became interested.

"To a school?"

"To school in Mardin . . ."

But then I thought, this would be impossible. The great King Darius could not start going to an elementary school in Mardin.

"Stop," I said. "We can find you teachers. One or two teachers . . . They'll teach you what you want. Things connected to life, to the century in which we're living . . ."

"Where would we find the teachers?" asked King Darius.

"I have no idea," I said. "But we can find them. We also need a wise man. Someone who will stay near you and analyze your life and what you learn."

"So I need a wise man too . . ."

"Yes, a wise man is necessary for you to maintain peace and quiet in your life, someone who will help you sift through all that you learn."

"Is what I learn going to unsettle me?"

"No, but it could exhaust you, make you indecisive; it can affect you. Actually, I don't know, Your Majesty," I said. "But someone has to analyze all of the things you're going to learn for you. For all the stones to fit properly in place . . ."

"For all the stones to fit properly in place," King Darius repeated.

Suddenly he stopped.

"What stones?" he asked.

"The stones in your soul . . ."

Alop the slave was by our side, listening attentively to all of what was being said.

I was standing there thinking.

Was it really necessary, I wondered, that King Darius learn everything that existed in life and that was talked about at that moment? Was it even possible?

Impossible, as far as I was concerned. Not just for King Darius but even for anyone who had lived in this century.

"You don't have to know everything!" I said.

"Why?"

"Because everything isn't necessary for a person's life and happiness, Your Majesty. Maybe you could learn the things that you like and that interest you, and improve yourself based on these things."

"Who knows?" said King Darius. "I don't know what there is; whether there's a lot or a little. I have no idea!"

He thought for a minute.

"I'll keep on with the television," he said. "As I look at it I see things and learn things."

"Well of course, keep looking at television," I said.

Darius pointed to Alop the slave with his hand.

The slave turned on the television with the remote he was holding; as he pressed the buttons the images changed on the screen.

The king asked me curiously:

"Who's this?"

"The prime minister."

"Who are these?"

"The beauties participating in the world beauty queen contest . . ."

"What's this?"

"A travel program. Temples in the Far East. Gold statues of the Buddha . . ."

"Who are these?"

"Football players, a football match."

"Who is this?"

"The prime minister again on another channel."

"Where is this?"

"The interior of a palace on a domestic TV series . . ."

"What are these people doing?"

"It's the program *We're Having Dinner*. I'll explain it to you later. It's a contest."

"Hey, what's this?"

"It's a marriage program, Your Majesty," I said.

"It's all so interesting," murmured the king. He was staring at the screen in astonishment.

The marriage program had caught King Darius's interest.

He said to Alop the slave:

"Find that man and woman from just now. It seemed there was some kind of agreement being made."

Alop found the channel where the program was being broadcast.

A man and woman were sitting next to one another on the screen. There was a screen with hearts on it between them. The woman would be considered middle-aged. She was overdressed, wearing a low-cut, blue summer blouse. She had black sandals with tiny black stones on them on her feet. The man was older. He seemed excited. He was wearing a dark blue suit. They were interested in each other, but they had not seen one another yet. They were exchanging questions.

The woman asked:

"How many children do you have?"

The man replied:

"I have two sons, but they're grown up. They don't live with me."

The woman asked:

"Why did you leave your wife?"

"We couldn't get along. We tried very hard to make it work but it didn't work out. I've been alone for three years."

"Do you have a house?"

"I have a house that I own."

"Retirement salary?"

"Yes."

The woman asked:

"Would you come from Boyabat to live in Istanbul?"

The man said:

"I would."

King Darius said:

"This is very interesting. A man and woman. Side by side. Let's look at this a little."

"Whatever you want, Your Majesty," I said.

The man on the screen spoke:

"What do you look for in a man?"

The woman thought for a moment.

"Fidelity, generosity, understanding," she said.

The man said:

"Would you think of living in Boyabat? I have a three-story house."

The woman replied:

"I might think of it."

The audience in the studio began to shout, "Open it, open," pressuring them to open the curtain.

The man asked:

"How many children do you have?"

The woman said:

"I have a daughter, she's married."

"Are you making it a condition that we live in Istanbul?"

"I don't know," said the woman. "I never thought of Boyabat. But a three-story house . . ."

The announcer intervened. He gave a lusty look toward the camera. She was a nice-looking lady, and it was clear he had enjoyed doing the program.

"Now I'm going to open the screen," he said. "So that Hikmet Bey and Şule Hanım can see one another. Let's see if there's any electricity between them! Are they going to go off and have tea together?"

Amid applause from the audience, the screen decorated with red hearts between the man and the woman opened.

Şule Hanım and Hikmet Bey looked at one another.

There was a silence.

Şule Hanım bent her head down.

"What happened?" asked the host. "Şule Hanım, what happened?"

Şule Hanım jingled the bracelets on her arms a little.

"I didn't feel any electricity," she said.

Hikmet Bey seemed to collapse where he sat.

"No electricity. I didn't feel anything," said Şule Hanım.

The host intervened immediately.

"Come, Hikmet Bey, let me take you over here . . ." If there were other contestants, he would introduce them and have them talk to Hikmet Bey.

"Sit there, please, Hikmet Bey. Şule Hanım, let me take you this way . . ."

The man and the woman disappeared from the screen.

King Darius turned to me in excitement.

"What's going on here?" he shouted. "The woman didn't want the man. The man wound up there all alone."

"Sometimes things are like this, King Darius," I said. "There's no electricity between the couples. Şule Hanım didn't feel any electricity."

King Darius said:

"What's electricity? The woman didn't like the man. She didn't find what she was looking for when the curtain opened. What a shame for the man. In front of everyone . . . and he says he has a three-story house . . ."

"The house is in Boyabat," I said.

"Is that far?" asked King Darius.

"It's considered far. It's far from the big cities."

"I understand, a house off in some faraway corner," said King Darius. "Women are like that," he added. "If that house were in a big city, maybe everything would have been different."

I looked at him in astonishment. He had immediately figured out what the program was all about.

"Man and woman," King Darius murmured. "They never change."

THE ZINCIRIYE HOTEL
MARDIN

I went back to my hotel room late at night. After asking the waiter for a myrrh coffee, I flung myself down on the couch with the silk pillows. I had tired myself out today; getting up early to go into the dream, and watching all those television programs in King Darius's palace in the heat had exhausted me. As I sipped at the coffee that arrived, I was planning to get into bed and have a deep sleep.

I thought about the salon of the Night People.

It was such an unusual place there. The old doctor and his friends . . . The things they talked about . . . the years not lived.

I was thinking of them as I lay there.

I had unlived years too. If the old men in the Night Salon succeeded in getting their unlived years back, I was thinking of applying to the same organization that they found.

What was being talked about was something between a dream and reality. I didn't take it too seriously, but then again, one couldn't be sure. It could be some kind of truth stuck off in some corner of life, hidden from the eye.

As I thought of these things my eyelids slowly grew heavy.

The instant I closed my eyes I saw Hikmet Bey before me. Hikmet Bey from the marriage program. He was wearing the dark blue suit he had on during the program. He smiled a little at me. I could just make out the gleam of a gold tooth on the left side of his mouth. It was a pained smile.

He was right in front of me. It seemed that he didn't quite know what to do.

He started to speak.

"I was humiliated," he said. "That woman humiliated me. I came all the way from Boyabat, it's my fault, and I went there in front of all those people. I'm ashamed in front of my sons; they saw the program. I don't know what I liked about that woman; then she said 'I didn't feel electricity' and I don't know what all, and humiliated me."

He took out small black worry beads from his pocket and began to tell his beads.

"Don't be upset, pay no attention," I said.

"Excuse me. At this hour of the night . . . Who knows what time it is? She touched my honor. What the woman said, that show, my wish to get married again at this age. It's my fault. Everything got to me all of a sudden. If I didn't tell someone, I would go crazy. Please, forgive me," he said.

"I understand you, Hikmet Bey," I said. "Forget about this. Everybody experiences things like this."

"I have to see her again."

"Don't see her. What would you do if you saw her?"

"I would say the things I couldn't say today. I wasn't able to finish what I had to say. It was left half done."

I thought of something.

"Go into her dreams. In that case, go into her dreams one night."

Hikmet stared blankly at me.

"What dreams? She doesn't see me in her dreams. She made me look like a fool in front of everyone."

"Go into her dream and talk to her," I said. "You'll feel better."

Hikmet Bey gave me a funny look.

"This is not something that's going to get fixed in a dream or anything like that," he said. "I couldn't tell her what I had to say. I have to go on that program again and talk to her again in front of everybody."

"How can we do this?" I muttered. I was sleepy. I couldn't quite concentrate. My eyes were closing. Hikmet Bey in his dark blue suit started to wave in front of me like the image of a branch in water in spring.

The door of the room slowly opened. I looked in that direction.

The Black Rose of Halfeti had come inside.

"Excuse me," she murmured. She made a move to leave.

She was very beautiful. Magnificent in her jet-black gown.

"Come, come in," I said. "Hikmet Bey . . . He has to go into a dream. Can you help him?"

"Of course," said the girl. "Whose dream is he going into?"

"He has to go into the dream of a woman called Şule Hanım tonight . . ."

Hikmet Bey was staring closely at this beautiful woman who had suddenly appeared in the middle of the night.

"Please come," said the Black Rose of Halfeti to Hikmet Bey. She turned to me. "Follow us with the seer stone," she said.

"Are you going to go into the dream too?"

"Since he's new I can't leave him on his own," she replied.

The two of them left the room together.

THE SEER STONE

I searched through my bag and found the seer stone. I was buried in the silk pillows. Very slowly I started to stroke the seer stone, turning it over and over in my hand.

An image suddenly appeared in the stone. I could see the Black Rose of Halfeti and Hikmet Bey quite clearly on the gleaming surface of the stone. They were on a side street, walking toward a twilight world. It was a place like the neighborhood down below here. There was laundry hanging from the windows. With no night breeze, not a branch was quivering. It was obvious that the air was as hot as blood. They had paused in front of an apartment house door now. The Black Rose of Halfeti asked Hikmet Bey something. Hikmet Bey nodded his head.

I was looking with great excitement at what I saw in the seer stone. They had to enter the dream by walking through the passageway and the aperture of the cockpit that was covered by a curtain. I wondered why the Black Rose of Halfeti had decided to try to go into the dream by such an unusual way tonight.

A little later I figured out what was going on. Hikmet Bey went into his house and quickly went upstairs and changed his clothes. Soon after that the light went out in the upstairs window and the man came downstairs. He had on a well-cut black suit and a new tie. The girl had waited for him downstairs. Suddenly I saw them in the passageway . . . Everything was happening very quickly. The young woman on duty said: "Come on, quick, the light went on! Be quick. The woman has taken sleeping pills. When she goes into a deep sleep, you can't get into her dreams. Hurry! Hurry up!"

With Hikmet Bey in front and the Black Rose of Halfeti behind, they pulled the curtain aside and dashed in.

The seer stone suddenly went dark. No matter what I did I couldn't get the light inside to come back. I was massaging it between my fingers, but it was pitch black. At one point I wondered if it had broken.

The stone wasn't working. I slowly put it down beside my pillow. This must be the magic of Mardin, the thing that had made it possible for me to have all of these experiences. I was vainly seeking to recapture the dream that had vanished inside the stone and bring it back.

Then my head finally drooped down to one side in exhaustion. I fell asleep.

LUIS BUÑUEL

When I slightly parted my eyelids, I found Luis Buñuel at my side, staring at me. I became excited and sat up. "Welcome, Don Luis," I said. "I'm going through a lot of things. Strange things . . . dreams. Entering and exiting dreams . . . Now I'm trying to solve the problems of a man called Hikmet Bey using the Black Rose of Halfeti. They entered a dream, and I was following it with the seer stone when it suddenly went dark. The dream vanished. I guess the stone is broken," I said.

"That's possible," said Buñuel. "I've never heard of this 'seer stone' before. There are magic stones like that in children's fairy tales . . ."

"But this is real!" I said. "It's like a little touch pad screen. It showed me many things."

Bunuel took the seer stone in his hand and turned it over and over.

"What happened to the old doctor?" he asked.

"He's in the Night Salon. He and three other men took refuge there. It's in Tunalı Hilmi, a place run by a woman," I said.

"You still have the erotic letter he sent you, don't you?"

"Yes. It's in my bag. Inside my business card case," I said.

Buñuel said:

"Look, look, there's something visible in the stone."

I bent down and looked at the seer stone. Hikmet Bey, the Black Rose of Halfeti, and Şule Hanım were in a narrow, little bedroom. Şule Hanım had been caught without makeup and her peignoir nightgown was sticking to her body; she looked older than her age. Her face was a little puffy. She was sitting on the side of the bed, saying something.

Hikmet Bey looked very smart in his black suit. He acted like he was a member of parliament. The Black Rose of Halfeti was unbelievably beautiful. She was next to Hikmet Bey. Şule Hanım was shouting, "What is this? What's going on? Why did you come to my room in the middle of the night? How much more can I explain to you that I don't want you? I just didn't feel any electricity!"

The Black Rose of Halfeti said politely:

"We're so sorry if we've upset you. We wanted to come into your dream. Hikmet Bey has something to say to you."

Şule Hanım, turning to the man, said:

"What do you have to say?"

Hikmet Bey gave a once over at the way the woman was sitting on the bed, her swollen face without makeup, her plump hands with no jewelry.

"I didn't get any electricity either," he said. "I wasn't able to say that on the program. So I said, let me at least get to her and say it to her face. I didn't feel any electricity from you either. Zero electricity."

He paused for a second, then added:

"Lose a little weight! The flesh on your back and waist is all dimpled."

Şule Hanım let out a shriek.

"You low creep! God damn you! So you throw stones at the fruit you can't reach, huh? You bum!"

"And it seems you have a big mouth too," said Hikmet Bey. "Good night."

He took the Black Rose of Halfeti by the hand.

"Who is this tramp?" shouted Şule Hanım. "In my bedroom . . ."

Her voice echoed out a little into the night, then stopped as though cut by a knife, and disappeared.

They came out from the curtain. They were walking in the passageway now.

Hikmet Bey said thanks to the girl. "That's a load off my mind. Besides, I was turned off from the start. She's just a crude, fat hag; she was after my house. Now I understand. My three-story house in Boyabat."

"Do you have a house in Boyabat?" asked the Black Rose of Halfeti. "Where's Boyabat?"

"It's on the Black Sea, a pretty little place," said Hikmet Bey. "It's a district of Sinop. Like paradise. I'd be happy to see you. Come and visit, I'd be honored to host you."

"Thank you very much," said the girl.

"My house looks out on Cripple Pine Park," said Hikmet Bey. "A person can relax there, as though you were in a different world."

They were slowly moving through the passageway as they spoke.

Buñuel said:

"What a fantastic scene. What happened? What 'electricity'?"

"The woman said on the marriage program that she didn't feel any electricity from Hikmet Bey. In front of millions of people . . . It hurt the guy's feelings. So he went into the dream and said what he had to say," I said.

Buñuel was laughing.

The seer stone went dark again.

"It doesn't show everything," I said. "It only shows parts."

"But it's wonderful," commented Buñuel.

He was holding the seer stone in his long, thin fingers.

"This is cinema," he said. "True cinema. It's as though it only shows the scenes that are full of emotion."

"Yes, that's right," I said. I was looking at him in amazement. He was holding in his hands the magic stone of the world he had himself created.

"I followed you," I said.

"When?" he asked.

"When the Black Rose of Halfeti went into your dream. You were standing there leaning against a beech tree. As though you were a part of the trunk of the tree . . . Suddenly it began to rain. The girl was in your arms. At that instant, lightning struck the beech tree. It reduced it to ashes."

Buñuel was staring at me.

"It was an extraordinary moment," he said.

"Love," he whispered. "Love . . ."

KING DARIUS

King Darius was filled with excitement. He had sent Alop the slave over early in the morning to bring me to the palace.

We were sitting across from one another, drinking our rose sherbet in front of that amazing view.

"The *Arena* program is on tonight," said King Darius. "Uğur Dündar's program. The continuation of what we saw last night. The 'Organ Mafia,' illegal kidney transplants, the kidney trade, and the kidneys removed from the dead bodies being prepared for cremation in the Indian city of Varanasi . . ."

"You know every detail so well, Your Majesty, you astonish me," I said.

"I continually watch that channel. They give out this information in bits and pieces. I kept it all in my head," he said.

Alop the slave bowed respectfully in front of the king.

"The time has come, Your Majesty; should I turn on the women's chorus, sire?"

"Turn it on, turn it on!" said King Darius.

The slave gently touched the button on the remote.

The Istanbul Municipal Conservatory Chorus and a Turkish classical string orchestra appeared on the screen. The women were very attractive, with rings on their fingers, pendants on their necks, and their blonde hair. They were rendering a song in one of the slow modes again.

King Darius followed them in admiration.

A slave refilled my rose sherbet.

THE PASHA

The Black Rose of Halfeti came to my room in the Zinciriye Hotel just about every night. She would suddenly appear in the dark of the night out of some shadow or crevice, and make her final preparations in my room if she were going to enter a dream, giving me information at the same time about dreams and people. I was accustomed to her now. She had become an indispensable part of the Mardin night for me.

She had a lot of work to do. She couldn't go into Buñuel's dreams very often. She was fixing her hair in front of the mirror.

"Spray a little perfume on," I said.

"Is it nice?"

"It's lovely. Put some on."

"Thank you," she said. She picked up the perfume bottle in the shape of a crystal ball that was in front of the mirror and sprayed a little behind her ears.

An exquisite fragrance filled the room.

"What is this?"

"It's the latest scent from Versace."

"It's wonderful."

"Where are you going now?" I asked.

"The pasha asked for me," she said. "I'm going to the pasha's dream."

"Is the pasha still imprisoned?"

"Imprisoned."

"When are they supposed to release him?"

"He doesn't know," said the girl.

"If you could only go into Buñuel's dream."

"I'm thinking of doing that tonight after I leave the pasha," she said. "I miss him so much."

"Ask the pasha. Have him let you go early."

"That's what I'm going to do. Okay, I'm going," she said.

The door of the room closed behind her.

The hot Mardin night fell wave upon wave on me, it seemed. I was left alone with my thoughts.

I picked the seer stone up in my hand and gently began to run my fingers round it.

The pasha appeared in the stone. His face was stern as always. The painting was framed with a carved wooden gilt frame. I realized that he was speaking with the old men sitting in the Night Salon.

Everyone was looking with great attention at the pasha's portrait from where they were sitting. It was nighttime again in the salon, which was illuminated only by a dim light coming from the lamp in the corner. The shadows were long. Outside, Tunalı was quiet and peaceful.

The pasha said:

"Seek your rights."

"We will, Pasha," said the old doctor.

"For goodness sake, don't give up your unlived years. Go after them," said the pasha. "If you have to, get a lawyer. Everything you need to do to follow up . . ."

"Look, that's absolutely correct!" Hıfzi Bey burst out. "Good for you, Pasha. That never occurred to us. If a man of the law defends our rights, we'll get results more easily."

"Well, of course," said the pasha.

Şevki Bey said:

"Pasha, I'm fighting back. I have a diaper, that ogre of a caretaker is waiting for me in the house, but I'm resisting. I'm holding on to the very edge of my life here!"

"You'll fight back, Şevki," said the pasha. "You'll fight on to the very end."

Mustafa Bey said:

"I can't quite make out the road that goes to Kızılay and Cebeci anymore. But I'll resist to the end. Roads and places are all mixed up in my head; it's all hazy, but I won't turn back."

"Are roads and places important?" said the pasha. "Pay no attention to Cebeci. Forget Kızılay. So what? What good does it do to the ones who do remember?"

"Right," said the old doctor.

"What good does it do the ones who remember, anyway? To remember the road to Kızılay . . ."

Hıfzi Bey said:

"So somebody goes to Cebeci without mixing up the way. Is this important? I ask myself. To get to Kızılay on the first shot . . . What does that show? Everybody's in Kızılay. Everybody's in Cebeci. But nothing happens. Absolutely nothing changes. I tried it myself."

"Yes, yes," said the old doctor. "These things are relative.

Somebody who can find Kızılay could get lost in a foreign country. Couldn't get around without a guide. There's no difference between someone who can manage these things and someone who can't."

"That is all exactly right!" Mustafa Bey burst out.

The pasha said:

"These things are all variable. See, you're gradually getting to understand that. Facts that vary according to point of view."

He paused for a minute.

"I have a guest," he said. "Take care for now. See you again later."

The seer stone had darkened. I put it on the night table next to my bed.

I was lost in thought. Was it really important if a person all of a sudden couldn't find his or her way to a place that they went to all the time, every day? Mixing up the roads, just being unable to find the road that leads out to the square?

Then to become lost, to become lost in the labyrinth inside and to have all the doors to the outside shut. Not to recognize, not to remember. No one, nothing. This was important, without a doubt. This, then, is the eradication of a portion of a person's life; perhaps, in some sense, a kind of freedom.

The conversations of the men in the Night Salon had a great effect on me. Their attachment to this life, to memories, to their freedom, and their realization that everything might suddenly vanish was an incredible thing.

They had all lived their lives one way or another and come to an end. They knew this, and they were resisting with all their strength, to avoid sliding down below.

The Night Salon was an unbelievable way station in the city and the endless night. I comprehended that.

My eyes were slowly closing. I feel asleep as the call to prayer was being recited.

BLONDE MESERRET

King Darius was scrutinizing the women in the chorus.

I felt that he liked one of them, but I wondered which one it was.

Alop the slave put the remote down next to the king's armchair. Darius said, as though he had read my thoughts: "There, the third from the left . . . She's so beautiful, so attractive . . . I'd like to meet her. I'd like to have her as a guest in my palace. Do you know her name by any chance?"

"Believe me, I have no idea," I said. "She's a member of the women's chorus."

"How can we get in touch with her?"

"I have no idea, Your Majesty . . . I'll try to contact the chorus," I said.

"Learn her name," said King Darius. "Let's invite her to Mardin."

King Darius was fixated on the blonde in the chorus, third from the left. She was a very attractive woman, singing the song with great feeling and closing her eyes at the end.

Little details like that must have captured the king's interest.

"We have to find her," he was saying. "I'll entertain her in the palace."

That night I was able to get in touch with the station after calling a whole range of places. Finally I learned the name of the blonde. Meserret Zumrut (Emerald). She was a former radio artist. They called her "Meserret Hanım from Ankara." Nobody knew who the women in the chorus were. The secretary I spoke to was devastated by the heat. She didn't know Meserret Hanım, so she must have been very young. "These are old programs from the archives," she said. "We put them on because it's the summer."

"If you could find me a telephone number."

"I've asked, but no one really knows. Call back in half an hour," she said, and hung up the phone.

A half hour later I was back on the phone.

The secretary had changed.

The girl I spoke to said:

"I have a very old number for her written in my book here. If you'd like, you can give it a try."

I took the number.

I dialed it nervously.

A sleepy, tired voice from the other end of the receiver said, "Hello?"

I introduced myself.

"Meserret Hanım, I hope I'm not disturbing you. I'm just a go-between. I had a hard time finding your telephone number. The Persian king Darius is a great admirer of yours and would like to invite you to Mardin, to his palace. He would like to entertain you and get to know you," I said.

On the other end of the phone, Meserret Hanım was flabbergasted.

"Who did you say?" she asked.

"The Persian king Darius."

"I've never heard of him," she said. "So he's a king . . ."

"One of the greatest kings of the ancient world."

"I understand. Thank you so much," said Meserret Hanım. "He's not connected with the Mafia or anything, is he? Please forgive me for asking. A person comes across such things in life . . ."

"Meserret Hanım," I said. "You're absolutely right in all your concerns. But you can relax. All it is in the end is just a trip to Mardin . . . They'll send you a ticket and meet you in the Mardin airport. You'll get to see this magnificent city."

Meserret Hanım said:

"I've never seen Mardin. I'll come. He's a real king, right?"

"He's real, it's all real," I said. "You know, nothing that exists ever disappears."

Meserret Hanım repeated what I said excitedly.

"Nothing that exists ever disappears from the face of the

earth. I think the same thing," she said. "Should I bring my microphone?"

"Please do," I said. "I'm having the ticket sent to your address. I look forward to seeing you here, in Mardin."

I took her address and hung up the phone.

THE NIGHT SALON

The old men who had been dozing in their armchairs in the Night Salon were gradually waking up.

The first rays of the morning sun had started to filter in through the curtains of the salon, and this world that seemed to belong to the seventies gradually started to become illuminated. The ceiling lamp had long since been switched off, and the smell of freshly brewed tea filled the room.

Şevki Bey said:

"Thank God, we woke up to another day; we managed to open our eyes."

"Amen," said the old doctor. "We're alive and starting a new day."

The blonde woman came into the salon.

"Good morning!" she said. "How did you pass the night?"

"We were fine."

The woman turned to Şevki Bey. "Şevki Bey, I put a pile of diapers in the bathroom; you can go and change whenever you want," she said. "If you need any help, just call me."

"Thanks a lot," said Şevki Bey. He got up from his seat.

The old doctor said:

"Throw away the diaper, Şevki Bey. Get rid of it."

"I'm still not so sure of myself," said Şevki Bey. "Maybe tomorrow . . ."

"What's the pasha doing, I wonder?" the doctor asked.

Mustafa Bey called out:

"Good morning, Pasha! How are you? You're awake, I guess. I wish you a wonderful day!"

The pasha, from inside the painting, said:

"Good morning to you. I've been awake for a long time."

The blonde woman said:

"I'm bringing a tea for you too, Pasha. I just made it. There are *simits* as well."

"I'll have a tea," said the pasha.

The woman held the tea in the thin-waisted glass up to the pasha's lips. The pasha started to sip his tea from within the painting.

"Should I give you some of a *simit*, Pasha?"

"I'll have it later," said the pasha.

The old men were talking among themselves as they sipped their tea.

Mustafa Bey said:

"I saw Kızılay in my dream last night. It was incredible. I went to Kızılay. Just like that. Without even thinking about it or asking the way. I found myself in the middle of Kızılay. I cannot tell you how free I felt. I went right into the Kocabeyoğlu Pasaj. I hadn't been in there for years. But in the dream, bang! I went in. It was very nice, even though there was nothing there for me. The bra merchants, ladies' underwear in all kinds of colors, slippers, towels, washcloths, tongs, hamam bath gloves, undershirts, slips . . ."

"What a world!"

"I thought I had forgotten those places, but I remembered all the details. Over by the bras, there was this hot number behind the counter . . . We were just looking at one another. I walked around in the corridor a few times. I was in a great mood. What a wonderful dream. I left there and took a turn around Izmir Caddesi. Then I went back into the Kocabeyoğlu Pasaj. The girl was still there. I was walking around in the middle of the bras. The girl and I came face to face . . . So that's it."

Hıfzi Bey said:

"I've been thinking about how to get to Cebeci since

yesterday. Over by Hamamönü. Old worlds. The old wedding halls, the conservatory building, everything's there. I know the way, actually," he added. "I can figure it out as far as Kızılay. After that it's a little confused . . ."

"We'll find it, we'll find it," said the old doctor. "We'll all go together."

"Oh, that would be great."

The pasha sneezed from the wall.

"God bless you, Pasha!"

"Thank you," said the pasha. "In my case, it's an allergy."

MESERRET HANIM

Alop the slave picked up Meserret Hanım from the Mardin airport and brought her to King Darius's palace in the Dara ruins.

The lady was in a state of great confusion. King Darius had filled the whole place with freshly cut roses and bowls of fruit. The rose sherbet that had been prepared was being specially cooled in the wind, and two female slaves were sitting in a corner, playing some stringed instrument that I had never seen before.

Meserret Hanım was older than she had looked on television.

The moment I saw her, I realized that the archive program they were always showing on television was very old. She had put on weight, but she was still pleasing, not bad.

She was observing in bewilderment this strange world she had entered, eating the fruit offered, looking out from the terrace in admiration at Mesopotamia spread before her.

King Darius was pleased. He had presented her with a diamond as large as a walnut. A room had been taken in the Zinciriye Hotel next to mine for Meserret Hanım. King Darius said, "So she doesn't feel alone."

I went back to my room in the Zinciriye Hotel late at night. I sat on my bed and started to play with the seer stone.

The seer stone was far more diverting than television. It was full of surprises. For one thing, there were no advertisements. There was no way of knowing where the image inside would begin and where it would stop. I felt that it could become addictive.

I ran my fingers over the flawless surface of the seer stone.

A huge, strong man suddenly appeared in the stone. He was young, built like a tree trunk, wearing a dark blue track suit. He looked carefully in all four directions as though he were seeking someone in the darkness.

He saw me. He started to run straight toward me inside the seer stone.

I had no idea who he was, someone whom I had never seen before. I wondered what he was looking for in the seer stone.

The man came close to me.

"I'm looking for someone," he said. "I wonder if you've seen them?"

"Who are you looking for?" I asked.

"I'm looking for someone named Şevki Bey," he said. "He's old. He's started to have a little dementia. I put diapers on him, I'm his caretaker, and he ran out of the house in the blink of an eye. I went out into the airshaft of the apartment to have a cigarette. If you ask me, he couldn't even get out of bed. So I went back in the room, the bed is empty; he split and left . . . I don't know what I can do. I looked for him everywhere all night, and I wonder if he fell into the hands of the Organ Mafia. He's an old man, he wouldn't understand it. He used to be very rich; they say he used to live a life of luxury. He supposedly has a mistress. His wife is still alive and never leaves the card table. One of those. A problem woman, with a cigarette in her hand. She has no interest in the husband . . . the son-in-law is very rich. He does work in Russia, in Ukraine. He's the one who found me. The daughter's in her own world. Right now she's at the summer house. The old man is alone in the house. Then I look, and whoosh, the bird flew away.

"I was really surprised," he added. "I put his water down next to him. I said, 'Let me go outside for five minutes.' . . . There you go, he's gone."

"I don't know anyone like that," I said. "I never heard of this family."

"They're very rich," said the caretaker. "I'm afraid that my man fell into the hands of the Organ Mafia during the night.

"Where else could this old man disappear to?" he asked himself. "Bye," he said to me. "I'm going to keep on looking for him in the night."

"Good luck," I said.

The caretaker disappeared into the stone.

Şevki Bey has to somehow get the news. Maybe the Black Rose of Halfeti would go into his dream and tell him how the caretaker is going all over the place looking for him in the Ankara night.

There was a tap at the door of my room.

"Come in," I said.

The door slowly opened. It was Meserret Hanım.

"I'm not bothering you, am I, at this hour of the night?"

"No, please come in," I said.

"I couldn't sleep," said the woman. "I couldn't sleep at all. This strange world I've come into . . . this unusual and enchanting city, King Darius, the palace in the ruins of Dara, everything has affected me in an extraordinary way. I can't believe what I'm experiencing. It's like they gave me a sleeping pill and I'm seeing a dream. What is illusion and what is real? I can't figure it out. You're real, I understood that. That's why I came to you. The king, his slave, that palace, that diamond as big as a walnut given to me, are all of these real?" she asked.

"This enchanting city of Mardin is real," I said. "King Darius, the slave, the palace . . . They're real too. Perhaps they're in a place where some other fragment of time meets up with this one."

"So these people are in a place where another fragment of time meets up with this one . . ."

"They're all real," I said. "If you open a history book, you can find the Persian king Darius right away."

"So this king exists."

"Of course he does," I said. "In the ancient world he owned everything round here; he was the master."

"Where did you meet him?"

"I ran into him here, while I was looking at the plain of Mesopotamia from a terrace café called the Seyr-i Mardin," I said.

"You didn't find it odd . . . ?"

"No, I didn't find it odd."

"That means it's real . . ."

"It's real."

"Where did he find me? I'm very curious. Where did he see me? How did he come to invite me here?" Meserret Hanım inquired.

"He saw you on television," I said. "He watches the chorus every day."

"I'm completely astonished," said Meserret Hanım. "What's a television doing in that palace?"

"I helped him get it. They came from Mardin Arçelik and set it up."

"Unbelievable," whispered the woman. "The ones they're showing are very old programs from the archives. They put them on for the summer season. Look at how much weight I've put on," she said. "The years haven't been kind to me. I'm wearing a corset. I feel like I'm going to faint from the heat."

She sat down on the edge of the bed.

"I don't sing anymore," she said. "My time is over. I gave up working in the chorus a long time ago."

"But in your time you broke a lot of hearts," I said, laughing.

"I did," she said. "But there's nothing now. I have nothing at all left. The other day I had a hard time finding money to get a permanent for my hair. I feel close to you, that's why I'm telling you all this. It's a good thing I got my hair done."

"Look, now you're in a palace in Mardin. King Darius is full of admiration for you," I said.

"Yes," she replied. "There are such strange things that happen in life; well, thinking about them is why I couldn't sleep. If only I were younger."

"What difference does it make?" I said. "The king is an admirer. And you're very beautiful."

"Thank you," said Meserret Hanım. "I'm very grateful, in the middle of the night . . ."

The seer stone suddenly lit up. A light like something from a shattered crystal flashed and then died.

Meserret Hanım cried out:

"What is this? It's like a treasure of light!"

Both of us were staring in awe at the seer stone.

The Black Rose of Halfeti had appeared inside the stone. She looked lovely, with her black velvet gown, her hair cascading onto her shoulders, and her ivory skin.

Meserret Hanım was taken aback.

"Who is this beautiful woman?" she asked.

"That's the Dream Woman. The Black Rose of Halfeti," I said. "She goes from dream to dream."

"That's so fascinating," murmured Meserret Hanım. "You mean a woman who ornaments the dreams of men . . ."

The Black Rose of Halfeti was all aquiver.

"Get yourself ready," she said to me. "We're going into the pasha's dream. He asked for us. He has to be at his best. He's going to go on Uğur Dündar's program, live."

"What time is Uğur Dündar's program on?" I asked anxiously.

"Tomorrow night . . . a doctor who does illegal transplants is supposed to speak on the program. The pasha's on during the political segment, and Uğur Bey's going to do a special interview. Why is he imprisoned in that painting? What's going on? Who listened to the pasha? An old diary that was found. Inside there were messages of love and passion. Uğur Dündar, he's going to ask the pasha about these things," she said.

"What is this diary?" I asked.

"That's why the pasha was arrested. Because of a love diary. Tomorrow night on the program he's going to talk about all of these things. The diary was found under the pasha's pillow before they put him in the painting. There are supposedly some reminiscences and letters of the pasha's in it."

"That's so interesting," said Meserret Hanım. "So the pasha was arrested because of a love diary. Who is this pasha? Where is he now?"

"The pasha is imprisoned inside a gilt-framed painting," I said. "The painting is in an old-fashioned salon decorated especially for old people. The salon is in Tunalı Hilmi Avenue, in a special place that shelters the Night People who have fled their homes."

Meserret Hanım whispered, "Enchanting, astonishing! Is there really a salon for the Night People?"

"Yes. It's on the first floor of an old apartment building in Tunalı. Four old men who are on the verge of losing their memory are holed up there right now."

The Black Rose of Halfeti said, "If you ask me, not a single one of them has lost his memory. They just can't find the way to Kızılay or Cebeci and places like that."

"They can't find the street?" asked Meserret Hanım.

"Well, of course they can't. They're old men who've spent all these years at home, growing old. Life has changed. Now they get the streets mixed up, but they all ran away from home," I said.

"Unbelievable things," said Meserret Hanım. "The pasha . . ."

"The pasha is incarcerated in a painting hanging on the wall of that salon."

"Come on," said the Black Rose of Halfeti. "Let's go in the dream. You come too," she said to Meserret Hanım. "We'll be back in twenty-five minutes. You won't be bored. The pasha's wonderful to talk to. He's seen and done it all."

"Come on, then," I said. "Let's go into the pasha's dream. We'll try to come back early to the hotel, right? It's very hot today. I want to relax a little."

"You'll relax, you'll relax," said the Black Rose of Halfeti. "Sleep until noon tomorrow. It really is very hot."

Meserret Hanım asked in astonishment, "Are we going to enter the pasha's dream?"

"We will, right now," said the Black Rose of Halfeti.

All of a sudden we found ourselves inside that passageway I knew so well.

"Come on," I said to Meserret Hanım. "Let's go that way. We'll go inside through the curtain."

The woman on duty asked:

"Are there three of you? That's rather a lot for a dream. You can't stay inside for very long. When the light turns green go in one by one. Don't make any sudden movements, don't get rambunctious in there."

"Fine," I said.

The green light went on.

The Black Rose of Halfeti went first, parting the curtain a little and slipping inside.

THE PASHA

I said to Meserret Hanım:

"You go in now. I'll follow you in."

I parted the curtain behind her and went inside.

The pasha was staying in a little room. The walls were painted white. There was a nice clean bed made up in one corner of the room with a bedspread on it. On the left side there was a little window in the wall. The room where the pasha lived was a plain, spare room for one person. He himself was sitting in the corner. When he saw us he stood up.

"Come in, come, please," he said. "What a lovely surprise! Three lovely women have come to visit me!"

The pasha gave the armchair to Meserret Hanım. The Black Rose of Halfeti and I sat down on the bed.

Suddenly I realized that the little window looked out on the Night Salon set up for the old men.

The pasha saw me staring at it.

"Yes," he said. "That's actually the place where I observe the salon from the gilt frame."

"That's so fascinating, Pasha," I said. "So you always follow those old men and the world of the Night Salon from this window?"

"Yes," said the pasha. "You could say that I'm in there with them. This world of old people . . . lives lived long ago."

"What is this 'Night Salon'?" asked Meserret Hanım with interest.

"It's a nostalgic salon decorated in the style of the 1970s that was set up in Tunalı Hilmi for old men who've escaped from home," I said. "There are four men there now, and each one's story is more interesting than the next."

"Did they run away from home?"

"Yes. It's a way of fighting back against senility and holding on to life," I said.

"That's so interesting," Meserret Hanım murmured. "Well, fine, but don't the people back home worry about them?"

"Some of them they're hysterically looking for and others, well, I just don't know," I said.

"There are even some people who are happy to see them go," said the pasha. "Life is a lonely trip . . ."

I nodded my head.

Meserret Hanım slowly went over to the open window and looked into the salon.

Excited voices immediately rose up from the Night Salon.

"There's a blonde in the painting!" Hıfzi Bey shouted. "It's just incredible!"

"Hello!" said Meserret Hanım.

The old men all shouted together: "Hello!" Then a great wave of excitement spread through the salon.

The old men moved their armchairs over to the wall. They were staring at Meserret Hanım.

Meserret Hanım suddenly burst out into song.

It was an old melody called "There's Another Chance."

The general said, "I love this song," and sighed. "I can't offer you anything here," he added. "I'm a prisoner. If it were the old days, I would treat you the way I wanted, to my heart's content."

"Oh Pasha, that's not a problem. Please don't even think of it."

"I'm going on television tomorrow night," said the pasha. "On Uğur Dündar's program."

"We know, Pasha."

"Will you wear a uniform?"

"I will," said the pasha.

Meserret Hanım was finishing up her song.

There's another chance
Do you say that it's only to die?
So what do you say, my dear
You're worth my whole life.

The song was over.

The old men in the Night Salon were in a state of complete excitement. They were on their feet, applauding Meserret Hanım.

Meserret Hanım withdrew back into the room, waving goodbye to them.

"Pasha, there's a journal. A diary," I said.

"Yes, there's a diary," said the pasha.

"They're supposed to talk about that diary on the program tomorrow . . ."

"Yes, Uğur Bey and I are going to talk about that diary on the program," said the pasha.

"Do you have the diary, Pasha?"

"No, they took it away from me," said the pasha.

"You wrote about your love in the diary, Pasha . . . that's what they say."

The pasha looked into my eyes.

"Yes, that diary was a message I left for the woman I love," he said. "I wrote everything in that diary, the things I couldn't say to her when we were together, the things I might have forgotten to say, everything," he explained.

"So you loved her that much, Pasha?" I asked.

"I loved her very much," said the pasha. "It's difficult for a soldier to express these emotions. But I wrote them down. I wrote everything in the diary."

"Then what happened?" I asked with interest.

"The journal was discovered and I was arrested," said the pasha.

"Why on earth were you arrested because of a love diary?"

The pasha chuckled.

"Not everyone can understand love," he said. "And in the days in which we live, who could possibly understand the love of a general? They thought about the book in a different way. It was misunderstood."

"My God," I said.

What the pasha said was truly confusing.

A red light above our heads started to flash on and off.

"It's time to leave the dream," the Black Rose of Halfeti whispered. "Come on."

She slowly stood up from where she was sitting on the bed in the corner. Meserret Hanım and I got ready as well.

"We'll watch you tomorrow night, Pasha," I said.

"I'll explain everything on the program," the pasha said.

I wondered who the woman he loved was. I hadn't had time to ask. A short while later we found ourselves in the passageway.

"I cannot believe what I am experiencing," said Meserret Hanım. "Everything is really very amazing."

A little later I dropped her off at her hotel room and then threw myself down on my bed.

The Black Rose of Halfeti was preparing to leave.

"Who was the pasha's lover?" I asked in curiosity.

"We'll find out tomorrow," she said.

She slowly opened the door and left the room.

THE PALACE OF KING DARIUS

We had all gathered on the terrace of King Darius's palace.

Meserret Hanım was sitting at the head of the group, and a slave would occasionally fan her with a dried palm frond.

The Black Rose of Halfeti had come with the Spanish director Luis Buñuel. They were sitting to one side holding hands. I noticed that Buñuel seemed somehow younger. He was smoking a thin cigarette as he looked out over the plain of Mesopotamia. Who knew what he was thinking?

King Darius was sitting across from the television screen. I looked for Silvia Pinal, but I didn't see her.

Another slave was serving sherbet and fruit.

King Darius bent down to my ear. "I'm going to hook up one of those coolers in the palace," he said. "The weather is very hot. We get exhausted for nothing. I wish we had gotten one that day . . ."

"I'll buy it from Mardin Arçelik tomorrow," I said. "They'll come and connect it right away."

Uğur Dündar's *Arena* program was about to start.

The remote was in King Darius's hand. After he ran through some of the channels, he turned on *Arena*.

Uğur Dündar appeared on the screen. As always, his tie and the handkerchief in his pocket were very elegant. Buñuel looked at him from where he was sat with interest.

Uğur Dündar said:

"Lieutenant General Gökdeniz Pasha will be here with you, ladies and gentlemen. In just a little while we'll have a live connection with him. As Gökdeniz Pasha is locked up in a cell, they'll connect him from where he is. We'll talk with him about the famous "love diary" that caused him to be condemned to imprisonment in a cell. As we know, this love diary found under his pillow had extraordinary repercussions and occasioned various analyses. In the end, it was turned over to a judge in order to resolve the romance that was discovered in this very controversial document, and the pasha was arrested and placed in prison."

The pasha appeared on the screen.

"Welcome, Pasha!" said Uğur Dündar. "You've been in prison for quite a long time. The love diary found under your pillow has given rise to a lot of speculation. In fact, the matter is so confused that even the High Council of Judges and district attorneys couldn't figure out what was written there. Everyone has a different opinion about what was written. Your diary has really become like a work of Shakespeare's. What do you have to say to us on this subject?"

The pasha said:

"I send my greetings to all the viewers from here. In addition, I send my greetings to the friends in the Night Salon who are watching us at this moment. Uğur Bey, my diary recounts a love, a passion. A kind of journal. There's longing there, hope, the pain of love, jealousy, obsession, who knows, even perversion. It's a document written for myself and the woman I love. Of course, when you start to seek military clues in it, a meaningless and difficult document emerges. I don't know why they looked at it like that. That's the true story."

"Fine, sir," said Uğur Dündar. "So then there's no password, no plan, no murder plot in what's written there, as was alleged . . . ?"

"A murder plot?" muttered the pasha. "I love her so much, that there were times I did think of murdering her. Her and myself. Like the House of Hapsburg. Like Rudolph von Hapsburg. It was so strange. Archduke Rudolph shot Marie Vetsera, the woman he was madly in love with, at the chateau at Mayerling, then he killed himself. That's depression."

Buñuel was listening with rapt attention to what the pasha was saying, once in a while asking the Black Rose of Halfeti a question in a subdued voice, and the girl would then explain something to him.

"So, there were times you shared the same emotions and anguish as Archduke Rudolph von Hapsburg, Pasha?" Uğur Dündar said.

"Yes," said the pasha. "But I didn't do anything. I expressed my love in the diary."

"And this book caused you all kinds of trouble . . . ?"

"Don't even ask," said the pasha.

Uğur Dündar continued:

"Thank you very much, Pasha, for coming on the show. You didn't let us down."

A commercial came on.

"Really amazing," said Meserret Hanım. "What devotion this pasha had! The man is wasting away in a cell. Who is the woman?"

"He doesn't say."

"It's a strange thing," said King Darius. "A tangled mess."

They brought new sherbets. Each of us took a sip from our sherbet.

A light wind sprang up.

A CONVERSATION WITH LUIS BUÑUEL

I had returned to my room in the Zinciriye Hotel. Meserret Hanım was in the room next door. We had agreed to meet for breakfast and then gone our separate ways.

Before Meserret Hanım went into her room, she commented: "That *Arena* program was fabulous! Aşık Pasha and what he said were just extraordinary!"

"Good night . . ."

Meserret Hanım went into her room. I heard her lock the door behind her.

I went into my room.

I turned on the lamp and was just about to fling myself down on the couch with the silk pillows when I suddenly saw Luis Buñuel. He was sitting in the armchair next to the window whose curtains were drawn.

He stood up when he saw me.

"I hope the hour isn't too late for you," he said.

"No, Don Luis," I replied.

"Please be seated. I lost sight of you when you left the palace."

"I walked in the ruins for a while," I said. "It's enchanting there in the moonlight.

"What can I offer you?"

"Thank you. I don't drink at this hour," he said. "I wanted to talk to you about dreams. A short talk."

"That's wonderful. Let's talk."

"You only know about the dreams of the middle and upper classes," said Buñuel. "Because you're around them. For example, have you ever tried to get into the dreams of impoverished people? Of someone completely different?"

"Don Luis," I said. "I went into the dreams of a few people I know, plus an old man and yours. To be more exact, I accompanied the Black Rose of Halfeti. I don't know very much about dreams."

"Who knows?" muttered Buñuel. "Maybe the dreams of forlorn wretches are completely different . . ."

"I don't know, maybe they are."

"The dreams of sick people," said Buñuel.

"Yes, the dreams of sick people . . . It could be interesting. Who knows what dreams they see?"

"I'd like to go into a dream like that," said Buñuel. "You know, to live there, to see what that world is like. What goes on in a world like that? What happens behind the scenes? I can understand people best from their dreams."

"I know," I murmured.

I looked at him in admiration. It was obvious that the subject of a new film was forming in his mind.

"Would you come with me tonight into a dream like that?" Buñuel asked.

"Of course I would," I said with excitement. "Whose dream will we go into?"

He slowly bent down to my ear. "Your dream," he said. "If you permit it."

I was completely taken aback.

"My dream?"

"Yes, your dream. I want to go into your subconscious tonight."

"But," I said. "It's like Mardin . . . Here, all these people, the different kinds of dreams, everything is my dream, Don Luis. As though they were all made from my dreams . . . King Darius, that magnificent palace, the Mesopotamia I observe from the Seyr-i Mardin . . ."

"A part," said Buñuel. "These are just a part of your dreams. That's right . . . but not all."

"Are you going to come into my dream tonight?"

I was very excited.

"How are you going to do it?"

"Go to sleep," said Buñuel. "Fall into a nice sleep. Then I'll gradually come into your dream."

My eyes were slowly closing. My eyelids felt heavy.

I softly buried my head in the silk pillows.

THE DREAM

I opened my eyes a little. There was a flash of light in my left eye. I lifted my head off the pillow in fear. A light like a waterfall flashed in the front of my eye again.

I was afraid. Trembling. I got up from the couch. It was as though there were tiny flies flying around in a cloud of air inside my eye. I tried to brush them away with my hands. They wouldn't go away. The flies I couldn't get rid of were cells whose shadows fell on my retina, clumps of protein. The back of my eye had torn.

I started to cry. Buñuel slowly came over to me.

"Don't cry," he said in a tender voice.

"I'm afraid. Very afraid, Don Luis," I said. "I'm slowly going blind."

"Don't be afraid," said Buñuel. "I know you're very scared."

"It's like a nightmare," I said. "I only have one eye, Don Luis. If I lose it, I'll never see the world again. That's death. Darkness . . . I'm very afraid, Don Luis. I'm in a nightmare. But it's a real nightmare. There's a danger of retinal degeneration in my left eye. A rip in the retina. I'm going to lose my mind."

"How did it happen?" asked Buñuel.

"I had an operation abroad," I said. "It was three months ago. The world was all clear and sparkling again. It was incredible! A person who hasn't lost his sight couldn't understand what I mean . . . I couldn't believe this shining world.

"My eye. What an amazing thing! A diamond that shows life to me.

"But now it seems I'm losing that diamond!" I said. I took him by the hands. I cried out with my last bit of hope.

"Help me, Don Luis! Help me. Light flashes . . . flies buzzing around . . . A person could go crazy.

"I may never be able to see the night again. Lit up screens, the faces I love, cities . . . moonlight. The worlds inside books . . ."

Tears were pouring from my eyes. A little light flashed again inside my eye.

"They can fix that," said Buñuel.

"How?" I cried. "How?"

I was inside a nightmare. I didn't know what to do. Every once in a while a slight waterfall of light flowed across my eye. I fled from the spots raining down and got myself out into the corridor. Like someone trying to escape a fire. I was struggling to breathe. Those spots of soot were in my eye; I couldn't get away from them.

Suddenly I realized in horror that this wasn't a dream. I was in the real world. Buñuel had disappeared.

I went back into my room. My hair was clinging to the back of my neck from sweat. I had to calm down.

"Relax," I said to myself. "Be calm. Nothing's going to happen."

I drank a glass of water.

"You'll get out of this. Be calm. Don't panic. Don't panic when it flashes. It might pass."

I was covered with sweat. I gradually stretched out on the silk pillows. I was afraid to close my eyes.

I turned my head to one side a little. I was praying that morning would come quickly. The flashes in my eye were gradually decreasing. The waterfall of light flowed across my eye again. It was diminished this time.

"I wish it were morning," I was thinking. "Just let it be morning right away. I'm so afraid, I can't close my eyes now."

"Where are you, Don Luis?" I shouted. He slowly emerged from behind the curtain.

"Well, you know everything now," I said.

He nodded.

"I know," he said.

"I fled and came here, to Mardin. A person alone in Mardin. Looking at Mesopotamia."

"You're not alone," said Buñuel.

"I don't want to think about that!" I forced myself to whisper. "I came here to forget about all of these things."

"You will forget . . ."

"But will I get better?" I asked. "I wonder if it will go away?"

He nodded.

"You will get better."

"Make a movie about the retina," I said.

I was exhausted.

"I made a film about the pupil," he said. "With Salvador Dali. A pupil being cut. People couldn't watch it. It's almost morning, rest a little."

"Don Luis," I said. "You know everything. You've learned all my worries, my fears."

"Yes, I did," he said.

"Please," I said. "Please don't reveal them to anyone else."

"I won't tell a soul," he said. "These are your worries, your fears."

I was crying.

"Don't cry. It's not good for your eye," said Buñuel.

He was telling the truth. There was a little flash in my eye again.

"Being blind is like being dead," I said.

"That's the way you feel now," he said. "It's a state of mind. You're going through something."

"I don't know," I said. "I'm afraid. Very afraid. Why did I have this dream? A nightmare."

"It wasn't a dream," said Buñuel.

I looked straight at him.

"How do you know?"

"You lived this," he said. "It's real. I watched you from outside."

"Really?" I said, despondently. "I wish it had been a dream."

"You're better now," said Buñuel. "Relax, try to sleep. There's still time till morning."

"What if my eye flashes?"

"Let it flash, nothing's going to happen," said Buñuel.

"I don't believe you," I said.

"Don't fixate on it," he said. He was preparing to leave.

"Sleep," he said.

He left the room and went out.

STARK NAKED

It was as though Buñuel had stripped me stark naked and left me lying there on the bed. That was how I felt when he pulled open the door and left the room.

Stark naked.

He had discovered my whole soul, my subconscious, my fears, the worries that I hide in the dark cavern of my chest. I was calmer now.

I had relaxed a little.

I slowly went to bed, stretching out on the white bedspread. I watched the first rays of morning light come in through the gap in the curtains for a while.

I had passed the night in Mardin sleepless and naked. A night alone with the flashes in my left eye, my endless worries, my fear. A night different from other nights . . . the night that the famous Spanish director Luis Buñuel came into my dreams and saw me in fear, weeping, nude.

A strange Mardin night. The back of my eye had calmed down now. I would never forget the nightmare that I experienced that night. I didn't know whether it was real or a dream.

I heard a light footstep. The Black Rose of Halfeti had come. She had her hair gathered behind her neck. She looked very beautiful.

"What happened?" she asked me. "Your face is dead white. Did something happen?"

"Is my face white?"

"You look very pale."

"Luis Buñuel came last night. He asked me something odd. He told me he wanted to come into my dream."

"That's so interesting," said the Black Rose of Halfeti.

"I closed my eyes. I felt a heaviness. I drifted off. Just then something terrifying happened. When I opened my eyes a little, lightning started to flash in my eye and black dots like soot began to rain down. I knew what this was. It was the onset of blindness. I began to cry. Buñuel comforted me. He told me not to be afraid. I told him about my eye and the flashes. He calmed me down. He saw my subconscious anxieties and fears," I said.

"Very intriguing," said the girl. "How is your eye now?"

"Just fine. It calmed down. There's nothing wrong."

"Forget what you experienced," said the girl. "It was just a bad dream."

"It seemed real to me."

"Don't dwell on it. I don't think it was real," she said.

I felt calm now. I washed my face and hands and combed my hair.

"Buñuel has a film like that," I said. "His first film. An eye gets sliced with a lancet."

"See, that's why you had that upsetting dream. A nightmare," said the Black Rose of Halfeti.

"Well, whatever, let's forget it," I said.

I had pulled myself together. I was ready to go out into the world again.

THE NIGHT SALON

Morning tea for the old men had arrived. They were talking to one another as they sipped their tea.

"It's light outside . . ."

"Thank goodness our eyes are open for another day."

"Now that you mention the word, my eye has a tick every now and then," said Hıfzi Bey.

"Do you have black dots flying around?" asked the old doctor.

"Yeah. They drive me crazy."

"That means the vitreous liquid has separated."

"What's going to happen?"

"Nothing. It'll go away in a while."

"Well, that would be good."

"Does it happen a lot?"

"Well, once in a while . . . It's like a flash of lightning."

"Let's wait and see," said the doctor.

Then Şevki Bey said:

"And I don't hear anything in my left ear anymore."

There was a silence.

"If we get the years we haven't lived back, all this will get taken care of," said the doctor.

"Right," muttered Hıfzi Bey. "If we just get those years back, there'll be nothing wrong with us. We'll all be fit as a fiddle."

Şevki Bey said:

"The first thing I'm going to do is go to Kızılay. Just stroll over to Kızılay."

"If you can get there, of course," said Mustafa Bey. "There's a haze. Something unclear somewhere . . . Like a kind of light mist . . . Like the fog on the road in springtime. That will go away, won't it?" he asked.

"Of course it will," said the doctor. "What is it, for God's sake, that cloudiness, that place where everything is just sort of unclear? What is it, for God's sake?"

"That's the lock to our brain," said Mustafa Bey. "That's just what we're going to open."

"The lock to our brain," murmured the doctor.

THE LOCK OF THE SOUL (THE PULL OF THE GRAVE)

I was going into the dream of the old doctor. The Black Rose of Halfeti came rushing to my room and told me that she wanted to say something very important to me in the old doctor's dream.

"Wait," I said. "I'm getting dressed. My hair's a mess. I must have had a flea crawl on me last night; my neck is itchy."

The girl leaned over and looked.

"There's no flea or anything," she said. "You have an allergy to that silver necklace you're wearing."

"Wait, I'll take it off."

I quickly removed the necklace and got ready.

"Should I put something over my shoulders? What's it like inside the dream? Ankara's cool," I said to the Black Rose of Halfeti.

"They say it's raining in Ankara, but I don't know whether that would come out in the dream," the girl said.

I wrapped a silk scarf around my neck and put on my deep red lipstick.

"Okay, let's go, I'm ready," I said.

Shortly afterward we were inside the passageway. I noticed there were a lot of unusual kinds of women in the passageway; some of them were smoking cigarettes, some of them had taken out mirrors from their purses and were powdering their faces and giving us a look as they passed by.

"We're going into the old doctor's dream, right?" I asked.

"As far as I know," said the Black Rose of Halfeti. "That's what they said on the phone."

I bent over to her ear, slowly. "These women are in line for the same dream. They're not Turks."

The Black Rose of Halfeti now scrutinized the unusual women all around us.

"They're Latinas," she said.

Most of them were young. There were four of five women in the passageway. Most of them would be considered pretty. They were like wildflowers.

We had come up to the cockpit.

A shiny, moist snakeskin covered the entrance to the cockpit. It was swaying slightly. The thing was alive. I suddenly realized that it was one of the most terrifying and at the same time one of the most attractive things I had ever seen. It was an erotic image. Spellbinding. It bore no resemblance to that kind of faded colored cloth that had covered the cockpit the other times.

The Black Rose of Halfeti, next to me, screamed:

"That's the door to Buñuel's dream! That weird snake. That pulls a person in like a magnet. That's the door to his dream."

The female attendant was standing at the cockpit.

"Whose dream are we going to go into now?" I asked.

"Luis Buñuel's dream," said the young woman.

"Oh my God, has there been some mix up? Weren't we supposed to go into Dr. Ayhan's dream?"

The woman looked at the screen next to her.

"Dr. Ayhan is awake at the moment," she said. "You were called for this dream. You know, don't do anything extreme in there. Try to speak in a low voice . . . the dream is crowded . . ."

"Who all is there?" I asked out of curiosity.

"Women who have been in and out of Luis Buñuel's life both now and in the past, some starlets, some extras he liked, a leading lady. A young nun from the Catholic church . . . That's the kind of group that's in there tonight," she said.

I slowly pulled the moist snakeskin aside and, brushing slightly against this slimy curtain, slipped inside. The Black Rose of Halfeti came after me.

We were on a dark road.

The cypress trees extending up toward the sky on either side off the road cut off the light, and there were some things swirling around on the creepy stone path in front of us, like little clouds with spider webs in them drifting around in a person's eyeball.

"What are these things that I'm seeing in front of my eyes?" I asked.

"I don't know," said the young woman.

We were walking on a long, narrow path in an old graveyard.

I had an enormous sense of fear and melancholy.

The sounds of a religious service came to us from a great distance, perhaps emanating from a church door that was left ajar.

"I feel the cold hand of death touching me," I said. "Let's run."

The Black Rose of Halfeti and I started to run in this old, weird cemetery.

"What is this place?" I asked.

"This is how you get into Buñuel's dream," the young woman said. "Maybe it's a graveyard from his childhood."

There were two dried flowers in the lap of a mournful statue of a woman. It was obvious they had been left there a long time ago. The colors were faded, and they lay there like old moth wings. We turned right at the statue and began to run with all our might. Suddenly we came to a flat place. A glaring white spotlight caught us and illuminated us. The light was blinding.

"Don't look at the spotlight! Run to the side!" a voice shouted.

We managed to escape from the white light and run off to the side.

Bang! We smacked into a bed. It was a wooden bed enclosed by Bordeaux-colored velvet curtains and a net. I saw Buñuel inside. He was leaning back against silk and velvet cushions, staring at us.

"Come in," he said.

We dashed over and flung ourselves on this unusual bed that looked like a board. The goose down mattress was unbelievably comfortable; the last time I had felt so comfortable at night was in a hotel where I had stayed in Moscow. I thought of that for a minute. The bed in the Crowne Plaza Hotel. Outside the lit-up Moscow night . . .

Buñuel said:

"Come over here next to me." He put one or two of the velvet cushions behind our backs.

"Your bed is incredible!" I said.

"It's from a set," said Buñuel. "It's from a set from one of the films about the bourgeoisie. It's very comfortable. I really like this netting and these velvet curtains."

The Black Rose of Halfeti was in Buñuel's arms now. Buñuel slowly kissed her on the lips.

"Where is this, Don Luis?" I asked.

"Madrid," he said.

The women we had seen in the passageway came in.

"There he is!" called out a girl with long red curls and black net stockings on her long legs.

She was pointing at Buñuel.

The women had all gathered around the bed emitting little excited screams. The net curtain opened a little. They were looking inside curiously at Buñuel and at us. One of the women started to scream.

"You cheated on me! I didn't forget that night in Mexico. You cheated on me!"

"Quiet, Maria!" said Buñuel. "Please be quiet. Don't make me regret calling you. Look, I wanted to see you. We're friends."

"Friends? What friends? I'm no friend of yours!" the woman shouted. "First Silvia Pinal, then Maria Felix. So now you're with this piece of trash?"

She was staring at the Black Rose of Halfeti.

Suddenly she took a gun out of her black patent leather purse and pointed it at Buñuel.

The other women started to scream.

The woman pulled the trigger.

We heard a deafening noise. Somewhere a window slammed shut. I looked at Buñuel; he had fallen back on the velvet cushions, covered with blood.

The Black Rose of Halfeti began to shriek a series of screams.

The women were all over the place. Maria began to run with the gun in her hand. She opened a door, ran outside, and disappeared from view.

The Black Rose of Halfeti was bent over Buñuel. She was sobbing.

"She murdered him! Murdered him!"

I was next to Buñuel. Slowly I raised his head. He opened his eyes. His face was filled with pain.

"He's hurt," I said. "We have to get him to a hospital right way. He's losing blood."

"Help!" the Black Rose of Halfeti was shouting. "Help! Call an ambulance!"

At the same time she was holding Buñuel's head in her lap.

"You will survive!" she whispered. "You'll survive, Luis."

The pillows were covered in blood. Buñuel's face was chalk white.

"Where is the wound?" I asked.

"I don't know," said the Black Rose of Halfeti.

We didn't know what to do.

The giant of Spanish cinema, the incomparable genius, was dying in the arms of the Black Rose of Halfeti.

"Ambulance," I started to shout. "Call an ambulance. Quickly! He's losing blood."

A worker from the set was hurriedly saying some things into the phone. He was in a panic. He hung the black Bakelite phone up.

"I told them," he said.

The women had vanished. We heard the ambulance siren in the distance. It was gradually getting closer. The siren was so powerful it could burst your eardrums.

"Don't touch him . . ."

"They're here . . ."

The Black Rose of Halfeti was crying. "I love you. I love you."

The ambulance had arrived.

Three ambulance workers carefully lifted Buñuel up from the bed and placed him on the stretcher on the floor.

"He's lost a lot of blood. Let's give him a transfusion . . ."

"The bullet went in from the shoulder."

They were talking among themselves. A light began to flash on the ceiling.

"The exit light is flashing," I said to the Black Rose of Halfeti.

"I can't leave him like this!" she shouted.

Buñuel opened his eyes a little from where he lay on the stretcher.

"Go, go," he whispered.

We didn't know what to do. The stretcher was placed in the ambulance and they closed the doors.

The ambulance drove away, sounding its siren.

The Black Rose of Halfeti was distraught. She was covered all over with blood.

"This is a nightmare," I said. "We went into a nightmare. Come on, let's leave."

I was very upset. Trembling all over. My nerves were shattered.

We started to run along the dark graveyard path holding on to one another. The wind had come up.

The deep green branches of the cypresses were waving, and the wind made a low roaring sound among the old gravestones and the trees. This was a different world within the world.

We were struggling to get away from there with all our strength. I came face to face again with the statue of the woman that had had the flowers left in her lap.

"We'll go this way," I shouted. "Otherwise we won't be

able to get out of here. We've lost our way among all these gravestones."

We started to run, hand in hand, to the right.

We turned and went around and came back to the same spot, as though the old cemetery had taken us in the palm of its hand.

"We're never going to get out of here," the Black Rose of Halfeti moaned.

"We will. Just don't let go of my hand," I said.

We were sweeping around in the deep, dark whirlpools of death. I realized that.

These aged, worn stones that hadn't been visited for perhaps half a century confused our vision, sending us strange signals from the other world; this Catalan cemetery was trying to pull us in like a suction cup. We were covered with sweat.

"We have to get out of here before nightfall," I cried.

"This is such a weird place!"

I called back, "It's a corner of Buñuel's soul, the fears of his childhood, and the weight of death that he feels over him. We have to escape from here!"

My foot caught on a stone.

I fell down full length. The Black Rose of Halfeti let out a scream.

My head was touching the earth. I had fallen on top of a grave. Out of the corner of my eye I could see little dead plants on the grave, the moss on the edge of the stone, and yellow marigolds.

"Get up! Get up from there!" the Black Rose of Halfeti was shouting. "The grave will take you in! Get up!"

With a final effort I managed to sit up. The sweat coming down from the roots of my hair flowed into my eyes. I didn't know that a grave could have such a powerful magnetic force. The earth stuck to me like a suction cup. It wouldn't let go.

"Stand up! Get up! Quick!"

I was able to get up to a kneeling position.

I read the name that time had begun to erase from the stone at the tip of my nose: DONNA ELVIRA.

The Black Rose of Halfeti pulled me by the arms with a last effort. I slowly drew away from DONNA ELVIRA.

I was covered with earth.

"I was dying," I murmured. "What a strange thing, I was dying . . ."

I had managed to free myself from the pull of the grave.

"Donna Elvira," I muttered.

Suddenly we saw the damp and slippery snakeskin slowly waving in front of us. We passed through it and ran to save our lives.

"We escaped," I whispered. "We escaped."

My knees gave way. I sank down in the passageway.

THE SEER STONE

We had come back to my room in the Zinciriye Hotel. The Black Rose of Halfeti collapsed on the couch and was crying hysterically.

"Don't cry," I said. "They'll save him. I'm sure of that."

"What if something happens to him?" she sobbed. "How would we know? They took him away in an ambulance."

"He'll get well," I said. He'll recover. I feel it."

She was in a terrible way.

I took the seer stone in my hand and slowly touched it. I was lost in thought. It frightened me to be that close to the place of death.

Human life is bound to a thin cotton thread. I felt that once again. We had run in the whirlpools of death and only managed with difficulty to get ourselves out of that deep, dark silent world.

The seer stone slowly started to light up. I looked at it anxiously.

The Black Rose of Halfeti asked nervously:

"Is there any news from Buñuel? Can you see the hospital?"

A woman appeared in the depths of the seer stone. She was an unusual woman, a dark beauty. She had a melancholy expression and a beautiful smile that added mystery to her face. I adored the purple velvet gown she was wearing. It was embellished everywhere with starched pieces of tulle and lace.

I had never seen this woman before. I looked closely at her.

"Who are you?" I asked.

"I am Donna Elvira," said the woman. "You visited my grave today. I wanted to thank you."

"Donna Elvira!" I said. I recalled the name that was on the tombstone of the grave where I had fallen.

"You were in that grave in Luis Buñuel's dream . . ."

"Yes!" said Donna Elvira. "That's a very old cemetery. Luis Buñuel used to play with his friends among the graves when he was a child, and this unusual world both frightened and fascinated him."

"Donna Elvira," I said. "We almost didn't get away from that grave today. We went down one path after another as though we were in a labyrinth. It was hard to get out."

Donna Elvira nodded.

"That's what death is like," she said. "It's very hard to escape from it. Different kinds of energy in the grave pulled you and confused your mind."

"That's exactly what happened," called out the Black Rose of Halfeti, who was sitting beside me. "My spirit was totally confused there."

Donna Elvira said:

"I'll come to you again. I'm being pulled back to my place now."

The image slowly began to fade.

A little later it had completely vanished.

Donna Elvira was gone.

"What an incredible thing," said the Black Rose of Halfeti. "The woman inside the grave you fell down on."

"Yes, an old graveyard that had a great effect on Buñuel when he was a child . . . That's how you get into his dream."

"We should have asked the woman about Buñuel . . ."

"We'll hear from him," I said. "Don't worry."

THE ROADS TO CEBECI

The lights had come on in the Night Salon. Outside, darkness had fallen like a coating of coffee over the city. Like a freshly brewed pot of coffee. Thick and moist. It obscured the Night Salon, these old men, and who knew what else. Underneath this mantle a thousand things were happening now. In fact, the interior of the darkness was teeming with activity; the night had thousands of invisible eyes and unknown ears.

Now was the hour of love, passion, and murder.

People who lived in flashing lights and shining worlds, who never felt the night or darkness, had long since merged into this multicolored night; there was sadness in dark corners and the lights had long since gone out in the houses of the poor. The streets had emptied and the police stations had turned on their dim lights.

Everyone was living his own night now. The endless terrifying night of the mentally ill and the brief brightness of a flash of light were very different things. The night had rocketed through the city from end to end like a bullet shot out of a gun.

Dr. Ayhan said, from where he sat:

"Years ago, when I was at Konak Maternity in Izmir, a woman came to the hospital. She had broken her ankle. I paid special attention to her. She stayed in the ward. She didn't know anyone in Izmir. What a strange woman she was. She had absolutely no connection to the city. A strange traveler, a peculiar stranger. I was very young. I fell for her," he said. "She had no place to go. When she got out of the hospital I brought her to my mother's house. Then one morning she ran off without leaving a single trace behind . . ."

"Allah, Allah," said Şevki Bey. "Who was that woman, I wonder?"

"Who knows?" said the old doctor. "I really wanted to have her. At that time I was like a spear gun. Twenty-six years old. The woman was older than me, but very attractive. I hadn't ever met a woman like her before. It was as though she had come from another world to Izmir, to Varyant. I caught her a couple of times staring for a long time at the Cordon bayfront in astonishment. Like she was seeing the world for the first time . . .

"Who knows what happened? Where did she go off to that morning?" he asked. "The one I'm in love with looks like her. Her eyebrows, eyes, the way she stands and sits. Just like her. As though I found her again years later."

"Life is so strange," muttered Mustafa Bey.

Hıfzi Bey said:

"Let's go out tonight and go to that Cebeci."

"But we'll get lost on all those confusing streets in the darkness of the night . . ."

"Why should we get lost, friend?" said Hıfzi Bey. "There are four of us. What one of us forgets, another will remember. Let's go to that Cebeci."

"Okay, we'll go tomorrow night," said the old doctor.

"No, that's no good; by not going and not going, we might wind up never being able to go at all," said Hıfzi Bey.

"He's right. We may never get to go to Cebeci."

"Well this is really terrible, then," said Şevki Bey.

"What's that?" asked the doctor.

"A lock on the brain," said Hıfzi Bey.

The blonde woman brought in their tea on a tray.

"I brought your evening tea," she said. "That's enough of these philosophical conversations."

The pasha was in the wall. He coughed a little inside the frame.

"Yes, Pasha," said Mustafa Bey. "Did you want something?"

"Come over here," said the pasha. "I have something to say."

The four old men slowly moved closer to the pasha.

The pasha began to speak slowly.

"The lock on the brain, the lock on the door," he said. "Both of them are awful. I have no lock on my brain, but my door is locked. So then I can't do anything."

The old men said to themselves:

"A lock on the door. That's an awful thing. You can't get out of a locked door. Even if you know the roads, it doesn't do you any good . . ."

"Oh, these are depressing things, locks, cells," said Hıfzi Bey. "Let's talk about other things."

"Okay, let's talk about other things," said Şevki Bey.

"Pasha," said the woman. "Would you like a sip or two of tea?"

"With pleasure," said the pasha.

He turned to the old men and said:

"And don't you make too much of a big deal out of going to Cebeci. You go from here to Kızılay, and then from there to the right."

"Is that all?" asked Hıfzi Bey.

"Yes," said the pasha. "Yes, that's all. From here to Kızılay, and from there to the right . . ."

"So that's the road to Cebeci . . . ," said Hıfzi Bey.

"Yes, it is."

"It seems so easy," said the old doctor. "Unbelievably easy. Why did we make such a big deal out of it?"

"Who knows?" said Hıfzi Bey. "We just did."

"From here to Kızılay, and from there to the right," muttered Mustafa Bey.

THE DAY WHEN THIS LIFE WAS NO LONGER MY OWN

Şevki Bey suddenly hollered:

"Listen to me!"

Everyone in the Night Salon was taken by surprise. Inside the painting, the eyebrows of the pasha arched slightly. The old men sitting in the armchairs in the salon were confused.

"Listen to me!" said Şevki Bey again. "I remembered. I remembered something. I remembered the day when this life wasn't completely my own anymore! I can see everything very clearly in my mind right now."

"What day was that?" asked Hıfzi Bey.

"It was the day when my caretaker really gave me a rough time," said Şevki Bey. "My eyes weren't seeing so well, and I wet myself. He came hulking over me.

"'It's your fault I got stuck hung up here. I can't enjoy my life, my youth, old man!' he said to me. He threw the soiled cloth into the garbage.

"'My whole life is cleaning shit,' he said.

"I was in shock as I listened to him.

"'But you get your money,' I stammered.

"'This isn't something you can just pay for.'

"'Then don't do it,' I said.

"'I'm hungry!' the guy shouted.

"For a moment I was afraid that he was going to do something to me. If he wanted to, he could easily kill me.

"I stayed quiet.

"He suddenly turned to me. Now he had a childish smile on that churlish face.

"'I shouldn't burden you with all this,' he muttered. 'It's not your fault. You're senile.'

"At that instant I felt like an ocean was welling up within me, horses rising up in the air," said Şevki Bey. "I needed him, and that was the terrible thing. If that bear knew my dreams, what I wanted to do, my desires, he would be amazed. The will to live got even stronger in me that night. I came and I'm going, but I'm still alive right now. I didn't want to see a lot or do a lot. I was a prisoner and he was the guard. I wondered how I could escape from this awful cage. To flee . . . to be free again . . . to have the courage to dive into life even though I'm a sorry wreck!

"The whole plan formed in my mind right then. I was going to get free from this clink, from this gorilla of a guardian.

"That night I ran away from home just before dawn," he said. "I made it. I wound up here. So here I am with you!"

He took a deep breath. It seemed as though he leaned back in the chair, where he had been sitting ramrod straight.

What Şevki Bey had said in such excitement affected everyone.

Mustafa Bey said:

"I had a guard too. It seems like exactly the same person."

"It's getting to be morning," said the pasha in a low voice from inside his gilt frame.

"There were many days when we felt that life didn't belong to us," murmured Mustafa Bey. "Days and years when we felt that life didn't belong to us . . ."

"As though they were both the same thing!" said the old doctor. His voice was pensive.

"Maybe that's what life is," said the pasha from within the frame. "Maybe that's the sum total of life. But leave it; don't think about these things now. You're alive now and you feel happy about that, don't you?"

"Yes!" shouted Şevki Bey. "I'm happy to be alive and to be here in this night!"

"There," said the pasha. "That's the other half of life."

The blonde woman came into the room.

"Let me turn on the radio so you can listen to it," she said.

The pasha said:

"Let's hear the news. The news."

The woman turned on the news.

Everyone in the Night Salon started to listen to the first news of the day.

"In the world today," muttered the old doctor. "Let's see what they say."

DONNA ELVIRA

"Don't cry, my dear. Don't cry anymore. Look, Luis is fine. His eyes are open," Donna Elvira was saying. She was stroking the Black Rose of Halfeti's hair. "He'll get better. He'll be completely well."

"Where is the wound?" asked the Black Rose of Halfeti. Her face was filled with anguish; her eyes were all swollen.

"He was wounded in the shoulder. He lost a lot of blood, but he'll get over it."

I was following these two extraordinary women from where I lay, looking inside the seer stone, which I turned slowly in my hand.

"Do you know him well?" asked the Black Rose of Halfeti.

"I've been watching over him since he was a child," said Donna Elvira.

"So you know what he was like when he was a child?"

"Yes, when Luis was a little boy he used to play in the cemetery with his friends. He was very naughty and impossible to control," said Donna Elvira.

"I've taken care of him since then. One morning he left white flowers on the grave. As though he sensed me," she said. "He was a very sensitive child."

I heard Buñuel's voice in the background.

"Have them prepare a painkiller for me!" he called out.

He was lying in an iron hospital bed. At the head of the bed there was a bronze crucifix on the wall.

His beard had grown out a little. His face was pale.

Two nuns in white rushed over to the bed.

"Where is Buñuel staying?" I whispered.

Donna Elvira said:

"In the Catholic Nuns' Hospital."

"How strange," I murmured. "As though he were in one of his own films . . ."

They gave him the needle.

Buñuel had turned slightly to the side now where he lay. The young nun at his side was looking at him with a mixture of admiration and affection.

"Do you feel well?"

"I'm a little better," said Buñuel.

The Black Rose of Halfeti jumped up from where she was sitting.

"I want to go in to him!" she cried.

"We'll go to him in a little while," said Donna Elvira. "He's going to sleep now."

And truly Buñuel gradually closed his eyes and drifted off into a deep sleep.

The nun in white bent her head down a little and looked at him.

"Who is this woman?" the Black Rose of Halfeti called out. She was in a rage.

"She's a nun," said Donna Elvira. "She's waiting to see if he has a temperature."

"How strange," commented the Black Rose of Halfeti. "This is a person from his own world. This nun in white . . ."

"Yes," said Donna Elvira. "There are always nuns like this in his films."

The interior of the stone became muddled all of a sudden. The connection broke. After I massaged it for a while, I put the stone down.

Luis Buñuel and the two shadowy women with him disappeared.

I stretched out on the bed. As soon as I did the stone came alive again. It was sending out a little light everywhere, like a nightlight.

I picked it up in my hand again.

The old doctor was standing in the center of the stone and he had noticed me. He took a step or two toward me.

"I left a letter," he said. "In the middle of the night, I left a letter for you in the mailbox at the apartment downstairs . . . I was curious if you got it?" he asked.

What could I say? I was overcome with surprise.

The old doctor was staring at me from inside the seer stone.

"I didn't get any such thing," I said. "I really don't know what you're talking about."

"Oh, so you didn't get my letter," said the doctor. He was confused.

"I put it carefully in the box. I understand. I didn't hear anything from you. I should have realized," he said.

Hıfzi Bey appeared inside the stone.

"Doctor," he called out. "Are you there, Doctor?"

"I'm here," said the old man.

"We're going to Cebeci. Tonight. Come with us."

"So we're going . . ."

"Yes, we're going. We made up our minds," said Hıfzi Bey.

"I'm coming," said the doctor to him.

He turned to me. "We'll see each other again," he said. "I'll write to you again."

"Good night," I said.

"Good night. Where can I leave the letter?" he asked. "So that you get it?"

I thought for a minute.

"Leave it in the same place," I said.

"In that white box at the young lady's place on the floor below?"

"Yes. Leave it in the white box," I said.

Hıfzi Bey called out from behind him:

"Doctor! Daylight is coming. Hurry up. We're setting out for Cebeci."

"I'm coming," the old doctor called back.

He turned to me. "We finally decided," he said. "We're going to Cebeci. We'll go by way of Kızılay. There are four of us. Each one remembers a part of the way. For better or worse . . . We decided to put our information together and go this morning."

I asked interestedly:

"Are you going to combine your knowledge?"

"Yes," he said. "We're going to put everything we know, everything we remember together and head off."

"To go to Cebeci," I muttered. "Why is it so important?"

"It's important," said the old doctor. "Because none of us can remember exactly how you get there. We can't figure out the way."

"I understand," I said.

"But we're four people now," he said. "We'll find Cebeci."

"I know you'll find it," I said. "I believe that. Have a good trip."

"Take care," said the old man.

He went over to his friends, who were waiting on the left side of the stone.

THE NUN IN WHITE

The nun in white had deeply bowed her head and was staring at Buñuel lying in bed with his eyes closed.

"What is this woman attempting to do?" asked the Black Rose of Halfeti.

The seer stone was in her hand. She was playing with it nervously.

I looked closely at the nun in white. She was young. Her face was very lovely. It looked like the face of an innocent child. Her long eyelashes cast shadows on her white cheeks.

She carefully bent down and brushed Buñuel's forehead with her lips. Buñuel slowly opened his eyes. Perhaps he was seeing the nun in white for the first time.

"Who are you?" he whispered.

"I am a nun from the Catholic hospital," she said. "Thank

goodness, you're conscious. You're speaking. I must tell the doctor this . . ."

"Why am I here?" asked Buñuel.

"You're wounded. You've lost a lot of blood."

"How did I get wounded?" Buñuel asked in astonishment. "In a duel? Or trying out a gun?"

"Neither," said the nun. "A woman shot you."

"A woman?"

"Yes. A woman from the old days . . ."

I only restrained the Black Rose of Halfeti with difficulty.

"Buñuel," she hissed. "This man is a lecher. Look, the nun's in love with him too. Look how she just worships him. What can I do? How can I get to him? How can I get inside this stone?"

"I really don't know how to get inside this stone," I said. "It's a strange kind of thing . . ."

"I have to get inside the stone. I have to get close to him," shouted the Black Rose of Halfeti.

She pressed the stone tightly to her chest.

"Buñuel feels me," she murmured.

Love is so cruel. I watched the hopeless struggle of the young woman at my side. At the same time I kept an eye on the interior of the seer stone.

Buñuel said to the young nun:

"You're someone I've dreamed about for years."

"Really?"

"Yes, really . . . a virgin, a young person who decided to spend her life enclosed in a convent . . . a lily condemned to fade in dark halls . . . an untouched virgin," said Buñuel.

The Black Rose of Halfeti cried out:

"Look! Look at what he's saying to that woman. That woman's in love with him. I have to go there right away!"

I was listening to what Buñuel said to the nun.

He was an ugly man . . . But he managed to entrance women. And then he would let them go.

I recalled Silvia Pinal. And now the Black Rose of Halfeti was at my side, weeping in despair.

"Perhaps one day," said Buñuel, "your virginity, the most valuable thing to you in the world, might you give that to me?"

The nun seemed mesmerized.

"I will," she whispered. "I will give it to you. It is the greatest, most irresistible desire of my life now."

The Black Rose of Halfeti let out a scream and threw the seer stone onto the floor.

I picked up the stone. It wasn't broken. But the interior was all muddled and the image had gone. It was as though some cloudy, filthy water were swirling around inside.

THE PASHA

The pasha was inside the seer stone now. He was shouting from the window in his cell in the form of a gilt frame into the completely empty Night Salon.

"They've gone! All four of them have gone! They went off to Kızılay to find the road to Cebeci!"

I slowly leaned down toward the seer stone.

"What could happen to them, Pasha?" I asked. "There are four of them. Nothing will happen."

"Are you so sure?" shouted the pasha. He had seen me. "Are you so sure? Their minds aren't set up for today. Half an ear, a quarter of a mind! Among the four of them they have maybe three eyes, two ears, and three hands and four legs in proper working order. Count them up yourself . . . They're exposed to every kind of danger!"

"The picture you draw is terrifying, Pasha," I said. "Three eyes, a quarter of a brain, four legs . . . It's a terrible thing. In other words . . ."

"In other words, if you put the four of them together, you'd only wind up with one person," said the general. "The four of them together make up one person. But it's very dangerous;

each one of them had a different dream, different desires, and fragments of different worlds stuck here and there in their minds."

"Yes, I see the danger," I murmured.

What the pasha had said was terrible. I felt depressed now.

"They're old," said the pasha. "They've run away from home. As I said, if you put them all together, you only get something like a complete normal person."

"This is very painful, Pasha."

"Of course it is," said the pasha. "That's old age for you."

"But they were talking very nicely here and explaining things," I said.

"They felt secure here in the Night Salon," said the pasha. "Outside is dangerous."

"What can we do?"

"I don't know. Try to follow them somehow," said the pasha.

"Fine, Pasha," I said.

The pasha had withdrawn into his frame and become silent.

KING DARIUS

"Let's eat, let's drink, let's have fun!" shouted King Darius, full of merriment.

He turned to Meserret Hanım and said:

"And you sing a nice song for us. Then we'll turn on the television and watch something."

Alop the slave softly said:

"Uğur Dündar is on tonight, sire."

"Is he on tonight? Wonderful!" said King Darius. "We'll watch his program."

I was unable to join in this happy and fun-filled atmosphere in the palace. My mind was on different things. The pasha's words seemed to be ringing in my ears.

"The four of them all together would only make up half a man. They're old, very old. They're near to dying . . ."

"What are you thinking?" King Darius said as he gently bent down to my ear.

Meserret Hanım had started to sing. Her voice echoed in waves on the stone terrace.

"Nothing important," I said to King Darius. "Something just came to mind."

"What is it? Say it, let us help," said King Darius.

"No, no, it's completely unimportant," I responded. "Something truly unimportant just came to mind."

"I wish you'd tell us," said King Darius. "Perhaps I can help you."

How could I explain to King Darius as he sat across from me in this indefinite palace in the night, in the ancient city of Dara, that four old men had run out of the Night Salon and were headed off toward Cebeci?

Everything was so mixed up.

Suddenly I realized what kind of confused situation I was in.

The Black Rose of Halfeti came to my room and was weeping there, demanding to go to Luis Buñuel.

"Well, let's get into his dream!"

"He doesn't want it. They're not calling me."

She started to cry again.

Buñuel was lying with his shoulder in bandages in a Catholic hospital, and a nun with an immaculate face, dressed all in white, was waiting at his side.

King Darius had bought a television for his palace, had had them put in an electric line to the ancient ruins, and a "global adaptor." He could see every place and everything he wanted and was amazed as he became acquainted with the world.

The seer stone he gave me was something incomprehensible. For me it was far more interesting and important than television. It seemed to show an image that was connected to the human soul. It encapsulated and reflected worlds that were suffused with emotions and illusions. I couldn't figure it out for the life of me.

The old doctor who sent me the letter in the middle of the night and his three good friends had run away from the Night Salon where they had sought refuge and were trying to find the road to Cebeci that they no longer remembered.

Meserret Hanım, a former soloist from the Istanbul Municipal Conservatory Chorus, had been admired on television by King Darius and brought to the palace.

The pasha in the gilt frame on the wall of the Night Salon was actually imprisoned in a cell. This clearly had some connection with recent events.

The solitary window he had to the world opened on to the Night Salon where the old men had sought refuge.

And I had gone in and out of any number of dreams. I knew all about the dream passageway, the cockpit doorway, and the warning lights in the dreams.

Outside, the Mardin night hovered over the plain like a giant space ship in all its incomprehensible beauty.

Everything was unbelievable and very beautiful.

The former king Darius was sitting next to me. His slave Alop was in the corner.

Everything was developing and moving forward in a bizarre way.

King Darius had the television remote in his hand.

Uğur Dündar's *Arena* program was due to start soon.

Donna Elvira, who had come from a Catalan graveyard, told me from inside the seer stone that she knew Buñuel's childhood.

One of Buñuel's old flames had suffered an attack of jealousy and shot him in his shoulder on the set. All of these incredible events had completely overwhelmed me.

If I go to my hotel room and try to think, the Black Rose of Halfeti will be there, clutching at me in tears, not giving me a moment of peace.

She was there at my side again.

"No matter what, I'm going into Buñuel's dream," she said.

"Don't leave me alone."

She had her mind made up. She was fixing her hair in front of the mirror. After she gave a little adjustment to the folds of her black gown with her hand, she said, "Come on. Let's go. We're going into the dream."

"Is he asleep?"

"Yes, at the moment. I got the news."

"Well, did he want you? How will you get into his dream?"

"He didn't," said the Black Rose of Halfeti. "There was no request or anything . . ."

"Fine, how will you get in, then?"

"We'll go the same way," she said. "I got special permission. Come on, let's go."

I got ready. We left the room together.

A little later we found ourselves inside that walkway I knew so well by now.

"There's nobody here," I said.

The passageway was completely empty.

"It's very close in here today," I said.

Yes, stultifying," said the Black Rose of Halfeti.

We were walking side by side in the passageway. A little later we arrived at the damp, shiny snakeskin curtain that covered the entrance to the dream. It was swaying gently, and an unusual odor emanated from it. It was a feral, attractive smell. I realized it was a male odor. The Black Rose of Halfeti was about to faint from excitement next to me. We carefully pushed the damp skin aside and entered.

The dark road lined with cypresses stretched out before us.

I felt stressed again. I felt like there was a cat sitting on my chest the moment I saw the old cemetery.

The Catalan graveyard was silent, as always. It was the silence of eternity. What were we seeking here? The branches of the cypress trees began to rustle in the wind. Suddenly I saw Donna Elvira's grave before me.

It was derelict, covered with weeds.

"Donna Elvira," I whispered. "Are you there, Donna Elvira?"

It was a silent grave, like all graves.

The roads in front of us became confused, and I felt a little sick to my stomach.

We heard church bells ringing somewhere in the distance.

Hearing a rustling noise behind me, I turned. Donna Elvira was walking a few paces behind me.

"Are you here? Donna Elvira?"

"Yes. I came to make sure you didn't lose your way," she said.

We had entered into Buñuel's dream. The cemetery abruptly ended and we found ourselves inside the Catholic hospital.

"There he is!" the Black Rose of Halfeti cried out.

I looked where she pointed. Buñuel was sitting up in the iron bed. The nun in white was fixing the pillows behind him.

They saw us.

Buñuel didn't seem very pleased to see us. The Black Rose of Halfeti sensed it.

We stopped where we were.

"It's always the same story," Donna Elvira muttered from behind me. "Luis is very lusty. Always the same story."

It was as though the nun had turned into a white panther. She had no intention of letting us near Buñuel.

The Black Rose of Halfeti said, "I wish we hadn't come. Let's go back."

"Okay, let's return."

We started to run.

We were in the graveyard again. The young woman was weeping at my side.

"To be in love is death," she said.

"Stop. Don't say such things. Let's get out of here," I said.

Donna Elvira disappeared between the twilight and the trees.

A CONVERSATION

"Then what happened?"

"Nothing."

"What do you mean, 'nothing'?"

"Nothing happened," I said.

I put the seer stone in my handbag. It wasn't functioning.

"What happened to Buñuel? Luis Buñuel?"

"I don't know. I never saw him again."

"Well, what happened to the girl? The Black Rose of Halfeti?"

"She disappeared. Probably she left. She must have had a really broken heart when she went."

"Well, King Darius, Alop the slave, Meserret Hanım? Where are they?"

"They're gone too," I said in a weary voice. "I went back there; there's no palace, and I walked around the ruins of Dara for a while in the blazing sun. I couldn't find the slightest trace of anything connected to them."

"But you experienced all of this . . ."

"Yes, I did."

"Well, where are they now? Where are all these people?"

"I don't know," I said. "Really, I don't know. I'm very sad. Sad because I lost them. What is this? What did I experience?"

"Mardin. The spell of Mardin."

"Why did it end?"

"Everything ends."

I was silent.

I thought of the old doctor.

"There was an old doctor," I said. "His friends . . . The Night Salon . . ."

"They were caught in Cebeci."

"So that means . . ."

"Yes."

"Where are they now?"

"They're in the old-age home."

"But they were full of life!" I exclaimed.

"Their brains weren't working quite right for this life."

"I get it. The pasha . . . ?"

"He's in the same place; he's not going to get out of there very easily."

The voice was drifting off.

I shouted out into the darkness in a last effort:

"Well, what was this? What was all of this? I lived it!"

"Life," said the voice. "Just life."

"So did I lose everything?" I shouted. "When will they come back? An old king, those sweet senile men who ran away from home, a beautiful girl, the famous Spanish director Luis Buñuel, the pasha in the gilt frame on the wall? A plump lady from the chorus?"

"They might come again," said the voice.

"And if they don't?"

"So what if they don't come? Were they here before?"

I thought that over.

"No, they weren't."

"Then forget about it."

The voice had gone away.

I felt a great emptiness and hopelessness. I felt completely alone in my room in the Zinciriye Hotel in Mardin. Not just regular loneliness, but as though a whole enormous world had slipped through my fingers.

I was pondering whether the world I had lost was very meaningful or not. Maybe not. A world composed of a few frequencies caught in the Mardin night. But for a moment, I thought, a very beautiful, very free world.

What had happened? Why had I suddenly lost it?

The old doctor's love, the four slightly senile old men attempting to go to Cebeci, Luis Buñuel, whose dream I entered, the lovely Black Rose of Halfeti, who came to my room every night. The crazy love she felt for Luis Buñuel. Our wandering around, going in and out of dream after dream, Mesopotamia stretching out to the horizon by day from the terraces, Mardin, whose lights turned into a flying saucer at night, the television that King Darius got for his place, his slave Alop, who never left his side . . .

These were truly very colorful and beautiful things.

Buñuel's falling in love with the young nun in white in the Catholic hospital, that old, forgotten graveyard we ran through when we were going into his dream, Donna Elvira . . .

I was thinking over everything. It was just as implausible that these things could suddenly appear as that they could suddenly disappear.

What had happened?

Maybe all of these colored dreams had been stolen from me. Someone could have taken them in the blink of an eye and hidden them in his own world.

I couldn't figure out what to do.

The loneliness I felt was indescribable.

My eyes continually searched in the corners of the room for the Black Rose of Halfeti.

She wasn't there.

She was gone, vanished.

I missed her querulous voice asking for Buñuel, full of desire.

King Darius.

How could he suddenly disappear like that? I'd gone back to the ruins of Dara so many times. The interior of the cavity in the wall was empty. There was no one there. A few little girls were selling wildflowers that they had collected.

The king's television . . . That had disappeared too.

Plump Meserret Hanım with the voice of a nightingale. Gone as well.

What I was really curious about was Luis Buñuel. That moist, slightly slippery snakeskin with its masculine aroma that covered the gate to his dreams . . . Where were they?

I couldn't enter into anyone's dream. It was obvious that I would never get to go through that passageway again.

I searched through my bag and found the old doctor's love letter.

I read it.

It was real. He had left it one midnight in the box at Elfe's house.

A letter inviting love . . .

Real.

So they caught the old men in Cebeci. I hadn't asked for the details.

I didn't know anything.

"I allowed them to be stolen. I allowed those incomparable dreams to be stolen," I thought.

Mardin had lost its significance for me. I felt my loneliness more deeply there.

Would I be able to find the world I had lost?

I wandered through the empty streets, fruitlessly seeking those intense bits of life in the paving stones, in the silver shops with their deep, dark interiors and tiny display windows, in the pictures of Shahmeran with her kohl-dark eyes that were pasted on the walls.

A PLUG CONNECTED TO OLD TIMES

The seer stone was in my hand. I was clutching it, but it was just a shiny stone: it may be the only thing I have from King Darius, the only thing that proved that King Darius existed, but it had turned into a stone with nothing inside, still, as though it had been unplugged from the past.

"What happened? What happened to all of them?" I asked in despair.

A voice at my side said:

"You found the answer yourself."

"I didn't find anything. What answer?" I asked.

"The plug was pulled out. You just said it, it got unplugged," said the voice.

In bewilderment, I asked:

"Was the plug pulled out?"

"Yes, the plug of the lamp that illuminated the worlds connected to all of these things was pulled out."

I thought for a minute.

"Was there a lamp that lit up all these worlds?"

"Yes. A lamp in your mind. Something like that," said the voice.

"It's incomprehensible," I murmured. "But possible. I hadn't thought of that. Well, if I plug it in again, would that lamp or whatever it is start everything all over again?"

"It could!" said the voice. "But can you find the plug?"

"I don't know," I said.

"It's not easy to find that plug, you know," said the voice. "It might be something a person only finds once in a lifetime."

"How is that?" I murmured.

"Life," said the voice. "Life is like that, isn't it? Can you easily find something you've lost?"

"I can't."

"Sometimes you spend a whole lifetime looking for it."

"Correct," I said. "But why did I lose those colorful worlds?"

"You didn't actually," said the voice. "They just faded away. When you go back to the big city you won't remember them."

"I can't forget them!" I cried. "I'm going to look for that plug. Maybe for the rest of my life . . ."

The voice was silent.

I called out:

"Answer me. Are you there? And who are you?"

There was no sound anywhere around me.

They started to recite the call to prayer from the Şehidiye Mosque.

I wandered around in the streets. I bought some soap from a

soap seller in the Gül neighborhood; I got some purple almond candy.

I went up to the Seyr-i Mardin and had a rose sherbet while looking out at Mesopotamia.

I waited there thinking that at any moment King Darius and his slave Alop would appear beside me.

The endless plain stretched out in front of me like an ocean made of earth and sand. I was gradually adjusting to this solitude. This was an old loneliness I was familiar with. A loneliness that often surrounded me, making up the walls of my life.

A loneliness that came to me at night.

It had come again. I ignored it. I got a plane ticket for Ankara.

I walked around in the streets of Mardin a bit more until it was time for the plane. Then I went to the airport.

THE DREAM

. . . In the night, I saw the Black Rose of Halfeti in my dreams.

"Come on, hurry up and get ready," she was saying. "We're going into Buñuel's dream."

I was flabbergasted.

"Where did you come from? How will we get into Buñuel's dream? What happened to the nun in white?" I asked.

"Just forget about the nun in white!" she said. She was fixing her hair in front of the mirror.

"Come on, let's hurry up. Let's get into his dream before he wakes up."

"How did you manage to set up the dream?" I asked.

"Donna Elvira arranged it," she said. "Buñuel wants to make up with me."

"That's fabulous!" I said.

I knew that what I was seeing had to be a dream. I kept my eyes tightly closed to avoid waking up. I felt happy inside.

I wonder what happened to the old men, I thought. I didn't believe that they had been caught in Cebeci and put in an old-age home.

The interior of the room was suddenly bright with moonlight.

"Where did this moonlight come from out of nowhere?"

"The seer stone started to work," said the Black Rose of Halfeti.

And truly, a white light was seeping out of my handbag and spreading out all over the room.

I immediately opened my purse and took the stone in my hand.

There were images appearing one after another in the stone.

Suddenly I saw the old men. It was nighttime around them. They were standing on a street corner, peering around.

"They're free!" I shouted. "This must be a street in Kızılay. Nighttime . . . So that means they got there!"

The Black Rose of Halfeti came over to me and was staring into the seer stone.

"There are statues behind them," she said.

I took a look.

"That's Güven Park," I said. "They got as far as Güven Park . . ."

There were tens of lamps lit in Güven Park, and the lights coming through the trees created an eerie atmosphere. The old men were sitting on a bench and relaxing.

There was a lot of night traffic in Güven Park. Narcotics sellers and women for rent spilled over a little into the outside world from the shadowy corners of the park. They made a dark, repulsive mosaic in the Ankara night.

"They made it out and they got to Kızılay," I muttered. "The pasha said to me that the four of them together would only amount to three eyes, two ears, three hands, one brain, and four legs. But see, they managed to do what they wanted . . ."

"Did the pasha really say that?" asked the Black Rose of Halfeti. "That's such a harsh description."

"It really is," I said. "A person grows and has the fragile evanescence of a moth's wing in his body and mind. Even a slight breeze could make his whole mind vanish and go away and his memories collapse into the darkness of his soul like a lifeless sediment."

"It's so sad," the Black Rose of Halfeti said softly. "You're talking about old age, aren't you?"

"Yes," I said.

"I'm ready," said the Black Rose of Halfeti. She looked carefully in the mirror on the wall one last time. She was checking to see whether she had lipstick on her teeth or not.

"Are we going?"

"We're going, come on . . ."

We started to walk toward Buñuel's dream.

So, there we were on those roads again. Those twilight roads lined with cypresses that seemed endless, that cold, old cemetery that frightened me, a strange feeling that there was no sound and no time.

Yes, we were moving through it all over again.

"These roads are so difficult," I complained. "The roads of a man . . ."

"The roads of a man?" asked the Black Rose of Halfeti.

"Of course, these are a man's roads," I said. "The roads that go to Buñuel. The paths of his soul . . ."

"I never thought about it like that," said the Black Rose of Halfeti. "You're right."

I liked the young woman very much and didn't want to disappoint her. Whereas I had had enough now of going into Buñuel's soul. The road both intimidated and exhausted me. I hadn't much of a chance of speaking to Buñuel.

We were walking along among the aged gravestones in the shadows of the cypresses without speaking.

Suddenly I saw him.

He was dressed in white, very, very tall.

I had never been so frightened in my life. For a minute I stood there frozen in place.

He slowly took a step toward me.

"Don't be afraid," he said.

A human voice.

I felt relieved when I heard it.

"Don't be afraid of me."

"Who are you?"

"I am Sheikh Ahmet Mardini," he said. "I came to tell you something."

"Sheikh Ahmet Mardini," I whispered. "What did you come to tell us?"

"Your period of meditation is over," said Sheikh Ahmet. "I wanted to tell you," he said. "Your meditation is over."

"What meditation?" I asked.

The Black Rose of Halfeti was also staring at this man dressed in white.

"Meditation," said Sheikh Ahmet. "Introspection. Withdrawal into your own world. Being one with yourself. Withdrawal . . ."

"Meditation . . ."

"Yes, you were meditating, and it's over," he said.

"So the meditation has finished . . ."

"It's over."

He was silently looking at me.

I was thinking over what he had said.

The Black Rose of Halfeti, standing next to me, said:

"Come on, let's move. We're late. Luis will wake up."

"We can't go anymore," I said.

She was confused.

"Why can't we go?"

"The thought is finished."

"The thought is finished?"

She was bewildered.

"Yes," I said. "Over."

Sheikh Ahmet slowly nodded his head.

"I'll go with you as far as Mardin," he said.

"We can go by ourselves . . ."

"I know, but let me come with you."

"Fine."

The three of us went back. The cemetery, the old, confused roads, and the dark-colored cypress trees were all behind us.

Someone called out to me. The wind carried a voice to my ear.

It was Donna Elvira! Her voice. I recognized her. It was like a voice coming from childhood.

I couldn't hear what she said because of the rustling of the trees. It got mixed with the wind and disappeared.

"The fall is dark here," said Sheikh Ahmet. "It seems winter will come early this year."

Halfeti's black rose was softly weeping.

"I'll never see him again."

"Who?"

"Buñuel."

"Why?" I asked.

"It's over. The thought is just over," she said.

She understood.

We came into Mardin with Sheikh Ahmet. It was afternoon. Everywhere was peaceful and quiet.

I took a look at Mesopotamia.

It was unique. It seemed to extend into eternity.

Sheikh Ahmet Mardini said:

"I'm leaving. I brought you here safe and sound."

"Thank you."

He became lighter and then transparent in a corner of the room, like a sheer curtain, and then finally vanished.

I sat on my bed. I wondered how long it had been since I came here.

What time was it?

What day was it?

It was as though I were slowly returning to life.

I was half asleep like a babe in the womb, exhausted like a woman who had just given birth. I slowly lay down on the bed.

The girl had gone.

I looked at the seer stone; it wasn't working.

I rested a little.

I ordered a rose sherbet. The waiter brought it. I drank it, sip by sip.

I waited, thinking maybe the meditation would begin again.

It didn't.

I realized that it wouldn't start again. I was like an unplugged television.

Burned out. Getting cold.

I carefully folded the airplane ticket for tomorrow for Ankara that I had bought and put it in my purse.

RETURN

The plane took off. I was leaning back, thinking of all the unbelievable things that had happened to me in this short slice of time in Mardin.

So I had gone into some kind of meditation. This city had turned me inward and made me experience all kinds of incredible things.

They started the service on the plane. I took a sip of my coffee.

I suddenly thought of something. I got so excited I almost spilled the coffee in the little plastic cup in my hand.

Sheikh Ahmet Mardini.

He couldn't have been a real sheikh. Where did he suddenly pop up from just at the edge of the dream? Like a movie character.

All of a sudden I thought how he looked like the priests in Buñuel's films. Long white robe, a pale face, those piercing eyes.

It could have been someone sent by Buñuel, this Sheikh Ahmet Mardini.

There was a strong possibility that he sent the sheikh to avoid seeing the Black Rose of Halfeti.

This last explanation started to seem very logical. It couldn't have been anything else. Why hadn't I thought of that before?

Buñuel's idea of a little joke!

That meant that everything I had experienced really did exist, that it was real and that world still went on.

I drank down my coffee. I didn't know. I didn't know at all.

I felt like I had come out of anesthesia.

I would wait.

Patiently.

As I had waited for everything all my life.

I had fallen in love with a city of stone, and it had made me experience unbelievable things.

I would wait.

A voice.

A shadow.

A breeze passing softly by my ear.

A whisper of love . . .

The evening sun.

A hand on my shoulder.

I would wait.

A letter . . .

14 NOVEMBER 2011
Ljubljana, St. Petersburg
Ankara-Elysian Pastry Shop

RECENT TITLES IN THE MODERN MIDDLE EAST LITERATURES IN TRANSLATION SERIES

Hend and the Soldiers
BY BADRIAH ALBESHR, TRANSLATED BY SANNA DHAHIR

Twenty Girls to Envy Me: Selected Poems of Orit Gidali
BY ORIT GIDALI, EDITED AND TRANSLATED BY MARCELA SULAK

A Portal in Space
BY MAHMOUD SAEED, TRANSLATED BY WILLIAM M. HUTCHINS

The Scarecrow
BY IBRAHIM AL-KONI, TRANSLATED BY WILLIAM M. HUTCHINS

What Makes a Man? Sex Talk in Beirut and Berlin
BY RASHID AL-DAIF AND JOACHIM HELFER,
TRANSLATED BY KEN SEIGNEURIE AND GARY SCHMIDT

Who's Afraid of Meryl Streep?
BY RASHID AL-DAIF, TRANSLATED BY PAULA HAYDAR
AND NADINE SINNO

New Waw, Saharan Oasis
BY IBRAHIM AL-KONI, TRANSLATED BY WILLIAM M. HUTCHINS

Lightning Source UK Ltd.
Milton Keynes UK
UKOW04f0119210717
305761UK00001B/8/P

9 781477 313091